PEMA'S STORM

DARK WARRIOR ALLIANCE BOOK 3

BRENDA TRIM
TAMI JULKA

Copyright © 2015 by Brenda Trim and Tami Julka

Editor: Amanda Fitzpatrick
Cover Art by Patricia Schmitt (Pickyme)

∽

This book is a work of fiction. The names, characters, places, and incidents are products of the writers' imagination or have been used fictitiously and are not to be construed as real. Any resemblance to persons, living or dead, actual events, locales or organizations is entirely coincidental.

All rights reserved. With the exception of quotes used in reviews, this book may not be reproduced or used in whole or in part by any means existing without written permission from the authors.

This trilogy is about sisterhood. To us, sisterhood is many things. It is a warm smile on a rainy day, a friendly hug, a cheerful hello...it's all that a good and lasting friendship is, only better. Sisterhood isn't just about blood. It's those women in your life who have shaped you into the person you've become. We love all the sisters in our lives!

As always, we want to say a heartfelt thank you to all of our readers who have joined us on this thrilling adventure. You have loved our Dark Warriors and we hope you embrace our young, energetic witches. They are a force to be reckoned with.

CHAPTER 1

A loud crash startled Pema, making her look up from her computer. Cursing echoed from the front of the store, and she cocked her head to the side, catching snippets of the argument raging between her sisters. Apparently, Suvi had dropped a box of fluorite crystals, and Isis was on the verge of going postal. Just a typical day at Black Moon. Shaking her head, Pema ignored them and wound her long blonde hair into a twist at the nape of her neck and went back to the papers she had been reviewing.

She didn't particularly enjoy the bookkeeping portion of their business, but someone had to do it. For two straight years business had boomed, allowing them to pay Cele, their High Priestess, back the money she loaned them. She had given them a loan to start Black Moon Sabbat, and it had taken a mere eighteen months to pay her back. They were proud of that fact, given the economy and Cele's astronomical interest rate.

More quarreling reached her in the back room, and with a sigh, she stood up. Time to play peacemaker. Pema was beginning to rethink her idea of opening earlier in the morning to service more of their human clients. There were too many nights they stayed up late trying to find the perfect martini. Prosperity came at a price, she thought, as she made her way from the office to see what had happened. But it wasn't like they were going to give up their pursuit of the perfect martini any time soon.

Glancing around the shop, she swelled with pride. They had built Black Moon from the ground up. The store was as unique to the Tehrex Realm as Pema and her sisters were. Neither should exist, yet they did and were thriving. Pema and her sisters believed the ignorance of their youth was partially responsible.

They were the youngest witches in the realm, and were impetuous enough to take the risk to create a business that brought humans into close proximity with the realm. They enjoyed interacting with humans, and thrived off of the unique verve for life they had. However, that didn't mean they were completely senseless. They understood the Goddess' edict to maintain secrecy, and would never do anything to risk exposure. But they liked to toe the line.

The pungent odor of lavender and jasmine claimed Pema's attention and almost knocked her over when she entered the front. She glanced around to see Suvi standing amidst a mess of books and various teas, with the pricing stickers in hand. She noticed the decks of tarot cards had already been labeled and set off to the side.

"What are you two bickering about?" Pema asked.

"We are too damn tired to be up and functioning this early, and butterfingers here, dropped a case of fluorite. The entire box is damaged. Thankfully, I managed to save the potions we made last night. Had she broken those, we would be looking at an even bigger mess," Isis griped. "I mean, seriously, those magics, if mixed, would be lethal. When we stay out 'til two or three, it isn't wise to open at ten." Pema pursed her lips at the familiar argument her sisters made to push back her new hours.

"But, you did save the potions, and this," Pema gestured to the mess around Suvi, "is nothing. We're a team, remember? We couldn't run this place without watching each other's backs. And, lest you forget, Suvi sells more crystals and leather pouches than the two of us put together. I'll bet she can sell the damaged ones, just as easy," Pema told Isis as she crossed the room and pulled Suvi into a hug.

"Ugh, whatever. I won't say I'm sorry to her. She needs to try and pay attention for once. All it will take is one serious mishap with our potions to prove Cele right, that mom and dad should have forced us to stay at Callieach Academy all those years ago, and I'll be damned if I prove that witch right about anything." Isis stomped to the big, wood bookshelves that had been in the Rowan family for centuries, irritation in her every step. Isis was easily upset, but Pema shared her disgust about Cailleach Academy. Pema never wanted to be under Cele's thumb again.

"I don't know why you let that female get under your skin. I don't like her, but I'm not going to spend my time worrying about her unnecessarily. I'd rather talk about Confetti Too opening tomorrow night. I wonder if the Dark Warriors will be there," Suvi sang as she flitted about, placing books here and there haphazardly. Pema smiled as she watched her sister, wishing she was more easy-going like Suvi. Everything seemed to roll off Suvi's back, barely ruffling her feathers.

"I'm sure they'll be there. This is Killian's club, I doubt they'd miss the grand opening," Isis offered with a sly grin, her temper finally cooling down.

"On that note, I'm going to change the stone on this wrap to a rose quartz. I want some lovin' in my future," Pema said, waggling her eyebrows as she crossed to the RockCandy Leatherworks display, glad to have the mood lightened. It was her favorite jewelry, and she always wore one of the handcrafted pieces.

"That isn't the right choice of stone if sex is what you want, sister. You need the red jasper. It stimulates vitality," Suvi commented as she walked over to help her pick.

Pema shuddered, Suvi was right. No way did she want love. Love brought nothing but heartache and trouble. "Thank the Goddess you are so much better at remembering that stuff than I am," she replied as she looked through the assortment of stones. "That could have backfired on me," Pema admitted as she unscrewed the rose quartz from the leather band and replaced it with the red jasper.

Being a witch and connected to the earth, Pema felt the power in natural objects like these stones. As the effects of the stone began humming through her system, she turned to the less pleasant task of cleaning the store. "Help me grab the ladder, Suvi. I want to dust the candles on the top shelf. Have you heard anything more about the updates to the club? When we added our protections it was all steel beams and brick, but I've heard it has a whole different feel to it, and that Killian hired additional security. That doesn't surprise me given the skirm attack."

Pema was going against her better judgment in asking Suvi to help her, but her sister needed a boost after the fiasco with the fluorite. As they reached the storage room and gazed at the tall wooden ladder, Pema briefly rethought her decision when she saw the shoes her sister had on. Suvi was always dressed to the nines, no matter what they were doing, and today was no different with her six-inch heels. She sent a silent prayer to the Goddess that they managed without further destruction.

"I heard that Killian had the council members send him their strongest males," Suvi shared as they maneuvered through the halls, "Of course, that means there will be new, highly-mackable males."

Pema released the breath she had been holding when they managed to make it into the open area without breaking anything else.

"Yeah, but can they dance? I'm ready to hit the floor and shake my thang," Isis said as she sashayed over to the stereo and changed the music to a club mix. Pema and Suvi started laughing as Isis began to bump and grind to the sound as she spoke.

"Stop shaking your ass and grab some black candles from the back," Pema told Isis as she climbed up the ladder. "I sold the last we had out here to Camelia a couple hours ago."

Isis winced as she headed to the back. "No telling what crazy Camelia is conjuring with them."

"I heard she was trying to bring her son back from the dead," Suvi said, handing Pema the feather duster.

"You can't believe everything you hear. She may be trying to communicate with him, but she's not crazy enough to believe she can bring him back, resurrection isn't possible." Pema figured Cele was spreading the rumor to discredit Camelia, given the bad blood between them. There was nothing worse than sibling rivalry, and Pema thanked the Goddess that she and her sisters were as close as they were. She reached over and the ladder swayed under her feet, so she quickly muttered a stability spell. It would hurt like a bitch if she fell from the very top.

"I know. It's as insane as what they say about us. I mean, we could never be part of a hostile takeover," Suvi replied from below where she was now rearranging necklaces on the glass counter.

Pema nodded her agreement as she ran the duster over the shelf and candles. "That's the problem with prophecies. They are vague, confusing—" She stopped talking when the tinkling of the wind chimes above the front door signaled they had a customer.

A cool breeze blew through the room, chilling the air. She twisted around to see the most stunning male walk through the door. He was easily six feet tall and had thick, brown hair that fell in soft curls around his ruggedly handsome face. He had a strong, square jaw that she immediately imagined running her tongue over. His warm, brown eyes invited her to share her secrets, and suddenly it wasn't so chilly anymore.

Her gaze traveled over him and she noticed that his jeans were tight in all the right places, and she could easily make out his firmly muscled legs. He took her breath away and she desperately wanted him.

Her sex tightened with need, and arousal flooded her panties as she was overcome with an uncontrollable lust for this stranger, and she couldn't focus on anything but getting him into the office for a quick tryst. She became light-headed when a feathering sensation in her chest set her heart racing. She wondered what was wrong with her. She was no blushing virgin, but she had never responded like this when looking at a male.

Reaching up to wipe the sweat from her brow, she lost her hold on the ladder. As she felt air rush past her, she never once thought to utter a spell. She blamed it on the fact that her brain malfunctioned from hormone overload.

Rather than landing in an ungainly heap on the floor, she was caught by big, strong arms and an electrical current raced across her skin the moment they touched. She wanted to climb to the top of the ladder to have this male catch her again. Then again, that would mean him putting her down, and she had no desire for that to happen.

"Are you okay?" His voice was gruff, and she loved it. The sound sent liquid heat spreading from her abdomen to her core and had her melting into his body.

As much as she didn't want to, she needed to put space between them or she was going to lose control. She pushed against his broad shoulders for him to let her go. She didn't fight it too hard when he refused to release her. "I'm okay. Nice catch, by the way. I'm not usually caught off-guard like that."

She should tell him to let her go. Her lips parted to say the words, but they were trapped in her throat. She breathed in his earthy, pine scent and a new flood of heat traveled through her. She needed to gather her senses, and added more force to her shove until he finally set her down. Her body slid down the hard length of him and she took a couple steps back before acting on impulse to rub against him like a cat in heat.

"I didn't mean to startle you. Are you one of the Rowan sisters?" he asked, holding out his hand. Did he crave contact with her as much as she did him? It seemed like an eternity to Pema since he had touched her, and she would die if he didn't touch her again. Okaaay, she was losing her mind and she needed to stop this behavior.

Her brain and hormones weren't on speaking terms, and she eagerly grabbed his hand and held it tightly. "Yes, I'm Pema and this is my sister, Suvi," she nodded her head in the direction of her sister, keeping hold of his hand. "And you are?"

"My name is Ronan Blackwell," the hunk said, keeping intense gaze into her eyes.

"How can we help you, Ronan?" Suvi asked, awakening Pema from her daydreams of ravishing his body. Realizing how odd it must seem to be holding onto his hand, she pulled from his firm grip and immediately felt a loss. She turned around to face the counter, needing to break eye contact with him.

"I'm not exactly sure. I need to win my female back. I believe her mother forced her to end things between us. I have never believed in this hocus-pocus shit, and I think it made her mother dislike me. I'm a shifter, and I believe in what I see in front of me," Ronan said. Two things happened. For a brief second, Pema wanted to rip this female of his to shreds. She quickly dismissed the notion, reminding herself that she was only fantasizing about the male, nothing more. And, who the hell was he to call their magic hocus-pocus shit? She swiveled and took in this alpha male, and his confident stance amped her body's response, making all other thought flee from her mind.

"I'm not sure what we can do for you. We refuse to make or sell true love potions, so we can't force this female to love you, and we certainly can't create a potion to make you believe in our hocus-pocus shit," Pema said, acid dripping from her tone. "Who is this female anyway?"

Ronan was quiet for several long moments while he stared right through her soul before he answered. "Claire Wells. Surely you have something for me. I was told that the Rowan triplets are supposed to be the most powerful witches in the realm. I want to convince Claire to follow her heart. She has loved me for almost two hundred years, and I don't believe that has changed." He moved closer to Pema as he spoke, angling his body toward her. She wasn't going to be a fool to think that he was as affected by her as she was by him. She was a means to an end for him, and she sure as hell wasn't getting in the middle of his relationship problems.

Still, Pema had to bite her tongue. This magnificent male could not belong to this particular female. She wasn't surprised that he was taken, but why did it have to be with Claire? The male was making Pema crazy with lust, and now disgust. Not a great combination.

She shuddered in revulsion. Claire Wells was Cele's beloved daughter, and Pema hated them both. She didn't have a jealous bone in her body, so why she was so upset over this couple was beyond her. Something had taken over her, and Goddess help her, she may embarrass herself yet.

Suvi jumped right into sales mode. "Of course we are, and if anyone can help you, it's us. We have several truth potions. And, if you want to remind her of the passion you shared, we have pink tourmaline to enhance libido," Suvi winked at him.

Pema watched their interaction, bewitched by his perfection and her desire for him. It had to be the red jasper messing with her. Her libido was working overtime with this male two feet from her. She needed to raise the price on these stones, and order more. This was obviously some powerful mojo.

Pema listened to him talk to Suvi and found herself wondering why he was with Claire. Those thoughts brought up the memory of her last interaction with Claire. It was the day Claire had moved back to Seattle, and Pema and her sisters were making their final payment to the High Priestess.

Claire stood in Cele's office with her hands on her hips, her long mousy-brown hair flying around her shoulders in agitation as she snarled at them. "No matter how much money you make at that store of yours, you three are still just the poor kids in rags. You'll never amount to anything."

Isis sneered back. "This coming from the one who relies on mommy for everything. We may have started in rags, but we aren't in them anymore."

A deep rumble brought her out of the memory. "Bag up whatever crystals or potions you recommend." That quickly, his sexy voice conjured images in Pema's mind of him hovering over her while he slowly thrust into her, driving her to climax.

She clenched her teeth together, telling herself that she *had* to stop thinking about sex. She unclasped the magnet of the wrap around her wrist and dropped the bracelet onto the counter. She walked a few feet away, placing more distance between her and the sexy shifter, and pretended to organize the tarot cards.

Ronan inched closer to her then stopped. He ran his hands through his hair, ruffling his curls and shuffling from foot to foot. His gaze returned to Pema's face again and again. Something in Pema stirred at the way he was staring at her. She couldn't decipher the look in his chocolate brown depths, but it was intense.

Suvi bagged several items for Ronan, telling him how to use each one as she took his payment. Pema didn't think Ronan heard a word her sister had said, given that his gaze never once wavered from her face. For someone who was so hot to win his girlfriend back, he sure didn't seem too concerned about it at the moment. That was *not* wishful thinking, Pema assured herself.

"I need to get to work, but thank you for the help. See you around?" Ronan asked, but didn't move to leave.

"If you are ever at Confetti Too then you'll see me plenty," Pema replied, hoping her invitation wasn't too blatant.

"I guess I'll see you often, since I've just been hired as part of the new security. Will you be there tomorrow night?"

"Yes," she nodded. "We wouldn't miss the grand opening."

"Save me a dance?" he husked.

"Dancing with me is certainly not the way to win back another female," she responded.

"You're right," he said. They stood staring at each other for what seemed like forever before he turned and exited the store. He gazed back at her from the street then hopped into a large truck. There was something about a male in a truck, Pema thought.

"That is some heat you two were throwing off. I need a walk-in freezer to cool down," Suvi broke the silence, fanning her face.

"Shut it, Suvi," Pema mumbled, staring out the window, captivated by glowing, brown eyes.

CHAPTER 2

Gripping the steering wheel as he drove down the street, Ronan was as shaken as he had ever been in all of his six hundred years. He had felt as if his life was over when he discovered his parents and siblings murdered by human poachers. The grief had been so debilitating that his bear had taken over. Claire had stumbled across him centuries later and spent weeks coaxing him back to his male form. She had been the single most important female in his life for the past two centuries. He had never imagined his life without Claire, and when her mother forced her to end their relationship, he had been determined to win her back. It was that determination that had led him to the last place he'd ever thought to go, a shop selling magical accoutrements. But the second he opened the door and saw Pema standing on that ladder, he felt as if the rug was pulled out from under him.

Now as he drove away from the Black Moon, it was taking all of his considerable strength to keep from turning around and seeking Pema out. He hadn't been this turned on in his life. His cock had yet to deflate and was completely on board with the idea of going back. The little witch was a vision and he couldn't imagine a more flawless female. Her long, silky blonde hair fell in loose curls down her back and beckoned him to fist the length as he took her luscious body. The compulsion to act on those urges was so intense that it was hard to focus on something as simple as driving.

Her sea-green eyes were entrancing, and it had been impossible to keep his gaze from her for more than a moment at a time. The most disconcerting was the electrical current that pulsed through him when their skin made contact, causing his heart to skip a beat. The experience had been so intense that sweat still beaded his brow. He couldn't make sense of the jumbled mess in his head.

He shook his head trying to clear it. He had gone to this magic shop to find a way to win back his girlfriend of almost two hundred years, and the bag containing the potion sat on the seat next to him. He should be planning a way to get it to Claire and resolve their issues, yet he questioned if he would ever even use it.

The image of Pema's mile-long legs encased in skin tight jeans flashed in his mind, and was only rivaled by the sight of her generous breasts straining against a green top that matched her eyes. When she had fallen into his arms, he found that her curves fit perfectly against him. She was, bar none, the most striking female he had encountered.

He was tied up in knots and the whole mess had him questioning if he was wrong about witchcraft. He couldn't help but wonder if there was more to it than lighting candles. The only way he could explain the way he was feeling was if those witches had placed him under a spell. Hocus-pocus bullshit.

He passed the Space Needle and pulled into a parking spot in the lot of the new realm club, Confetti Too. As he put the truck in park and looked at the warehouse, he forced thoughts of Pema from his mind and focused on work.

Hayden, the shifter Omega, had personally recruited Ronan to protect the realm nightclub. For some time, Ronan had wanted to make a difference in his world. He wanted to be part of something more important than merely throwing around drunken shifters, and the skirm activity in Seattle had convinced him to accept the position, despite the fact that he would be closer to Claire's mother.

He climbed out of the car and adjusted his erection before heading into the building where he encountered the chaos of last-minute preparations for the opening the next night. He spotted Killian talking to one of the waitresses and headed over.

Ronan waited while Kill gave the nymph instructions and tried to keep his mind off Pema, but the witch back at the candle shop continued to consume his thoughts. Of one thing he was certain. He had never before wanted a female as fervently as he wanted Pema.

"What do you want me to do today?" Ronan asked, feeling his anger rise to mask his confusion and frustration. Like many males, anger was his go-to emotion. Anger was easier to express than it was for him to deal with the situation he suddenly found himself in.

"You can start by chilling a bit, buddy. Tensions are high enough here with the Grand Opening tomorrow night." His boss eyed him intently, "Okay, what's up? You're edgy." Kill never missed a thing, but no way in hell was Ronan going to tell him about his new obsession with the alluring Pema. Ronan was beginning to feel like a female, he'd spent five minutes with her and he needed to get over it. He reminded himself that he was in love with Claire and determined to win her back.

"Sorry, this morning turned to shit. I'm good," Ronan tried to reassure his boss.

"No, you're not good. Your bear is itching to break through. Your eyes are completely black and your claws are out," Kill pointed out. Ronan looked down and realized he was right. He'd been so preoccupied that he wasn't aware his animal was so close to the surface. His bear had never been this restless unless Ronan was ready to beat the shit of out someone.

"I can call Hayden over if you need help regaining control. The grand opening is tomorrow night and I need you on your A-game. You came from a small town, and tomorrow night there will be twice as many people here as you've ever seen in one place. Hayden assured me that you were the male for the job. Was he wrong?" Killian asked, eyeing him closely.

"No, he wasn't wrong. I thrive in chaos. Don't worry about me, I'll be fine," Ronan reassured the sorcerer. He took several deep breaths until his claws retracted.

"Then it must be about a woman," Kill laughed.

Ronan felt his cheeks warm. Now he was fucking blushing? If he didn't watch it, this was going to ruin his image. "Claire dumped me," he told his boss, unsure why he was now sharing it with him. He wasn't one to talk about his relationship with anyone, let alone someone he hadn't known very long. "I went to Black Moon Sabbat looking for answers but...question, what's the story on witches and their magic?"

Kill winced and leaned back against the bar. "Claire dumped you, and you go to Black Moon? I hope you didn't go to Black Moon to win her back because that is going to piss her off when she hears about it. And you don't want to mess with the Wells family."

Ronan crossed his arms over his massive chest and pondered the sorcerer's words. He'd never even heard of Pema and her sisters until he had asked a co-worker where he should go for help with a witch. "Why? What's the deal with her and Black Moon?"

Killian sucked in a breath and let it out in a hiss. "As you know, the Wells are the ruling family of the witches, which means they are very powerful. There is a prophecy that most believe refers to the Rowan triplets and a shift in power. Put simply, the Rowans and Wells are a volatile mix. If their magic clashes, you want to be very far away."

"What's the worst they could do? Kill me with a love potion? Magic isn't capable of causing real harm."

Killian barked out a laugh. "That's like me saying a male can't change into a bear. Magic is an elemental force in our world that shapes all aspects of our lives," Kill shook his head. "You've lived with Claire for over a hundred years. Either she has kept her talents secret or you have spent too much time cooped up with shifters. There is more out there than you realize." The sorcerer splayed his fingers and muttered a word in a foreign language. Blue light sparked between his fingertips.

Wow, Ronan thought, not impressed. He could do a great light show, with shadow animals on the wall and everything.

Ronan was about to ask Killian to make a bear shape on the wall when he felt a tightening in his throat. Before he knew it, he was unable to breathe and clutched at his throat. He could hold his breath for several minutes, but when the pressure steadily increased, he panicked.

There were invisible hands around his throat, strangling the life out of him. When spots dotted his vision, his bear began clamoring underneath his skin. His fingers clawed at his throat in an attempt to get air, but all he managed was to leave bleeding furrows. Goddess help Killian's new club, his bear was going to break through soon and go on a rampage.

Killian muttered another foreign word and closed his hands into fists. Instantly, the pressure was relieved, leaving Ronan gasping for a lungful of air. Heaving, he glared at his boss. "What the hell?"

Killian had a smug look on his face that Ronan wanted to wipe away with his fists. With power like that, there was a reason for the male to be so confidant. It made Ronan wonder how skirm had been able to best Killian and the Dark Warriors in the battle that destroyed the original Club Confetti.

"That was a simple strangulation spell. Now do you believe in the power of magic?"

"Fuck you," he gasped.

"I'll take that as a yes. Believe me, that's nothing compared to what will happen if you cross the Wells. Claire is Cele's only child and Cele is the High Priestess in the realm. Cele rules the witches for a reason. Individually, she is the most powerful witch in the realm. Her position is on par with Hayden, Dante, Zander, and Evzen."

All members of the Tehrex Realm knew who the faction leaders were, Ronan just had never seen Claire's mother in the same league as these males. It made him wonder why Cele had chosen not to be a part of the Dark Alliance council.

Ronan rubbed his sore throat. "Thanks. I'll keep that in mind, but if you ever do that to me again, I'll kick your ass. Now, what can I do to help get things ready for tomorrow night?"

Killian laughed and rattled off a list of tasks. Ronan's mind returned to Pema and her strawberry scent. She would be sweet and succulent. In fact, everything about this female was already branded into his memory. He forced his mind to focus on what Killian needed him to do rather than how badly he wanted to seek Pema out and take a taste.

∽

Pema ran a rag over the glass for the umpteenth time. She had been cleaning the countertop for the past hour, unable to stop daydreaming about the ruggedly-handsome Ronan. Despite the incense burning, all she could smell was his tantalizing, masculine musk. Her sisters had teased her relentlessly.

Suvi had laughed herself silly while Isis had been pissed at her for wanting what they had called Claire's leftovers. Pema would have been bothered by their taunts, but they hadn't said anything that wasn't true. She was obsessing over the male and didn't understand why she was unable to push thoughts of him from her mind.

Surely he wasn't as sexy as her mind was telling her. The next time she saw him, her fantasy would be shattered; reality was never as good as fantasy.

For the hundredth time that day, the wind chime tinkled above the door and her head snapped up, hoping it was him. Her heart stopped and her mouth dropped open when he stopped in the entry, holding the door open. Their gazes met and locked.

He was back, and she had been dead wrong. Reality was so much better than fantasy. He was by far the sexiest male ever created. She stood there gaping like an idiot, unable to tear her eyes from his. She felt her arousal spike, and a small smile curved her mouth when she saw the telltale-

glow in his eyes that told her he was just as affected by her as she was by him.

The clearing of a throat interrupted the moment. Pema broke eye contact to glare a warning at her sister. "We didn't officially meet earlier. I'm Isis, Pema's sister," Isis said, holding her hand out to shake his.

Pema watched as he let go of the door and let it shut quietly behind him. The light coming through the windows at this time of day highlighted his body to perfection. The sun paid homage to his God-like physique. She told herself she was being pathetic when she missed his warm gaze as he turned to greet her sister. "I'm Ronan. It's nice to meet you." Pema refused to acknowledge that she was jealous her sister was touching him.

Suvi sidled up next to Pema. "It's good to see you again. Some of us are more excited than others," Suvi smiled. Pema barely held back from hitting Suvi. "How can we help you this time?"

Ronan once again turned that magnetic gaze to Pema, ignoring Suvi completely. "I was hoping we could talk in private, Pema." Goddess, his voice made her quake in her boots. And the way his tongue curled around her name had her flushing and praying that his version of talk including suckling her breasts and moist, feminine flesh. She needed to get ahold of herself. She had never lost her mind over a good-looking male before, and she wasn't about to start now.

She cleared her throat of its dryness and found her voice. "Uh, yeah, sure. We have an office in the back. Follow me," she motioned to the hallway and started walking. The heat of his gaze burned like a brand on her backside and he followed behind.

She entered the cluttered room and decided test the

water. "Before you say anything, I want you to know that I hope you can work it out with Claire," she told him as she crossed toward the desk.

"Do you really?" he asked quietly. The heat burning in his gaze made her want to shed her clothes. Instead, she walked to the other side of the desk, putting space and furniture between them. He may still get back together with Claire, so he was off-limits.

As Pema tried to decipher his emotions from his facial expressions, she wondered why it was so hard for her to tell him yes, she wanted them to get back together. "Why wouldn't I? I have nothing against Claire, despite who her mother is. Okay, I'll admit that I don't like her, but if she's what floats your boat..." she trailed off meaningfully.

"A day ago I'd have said yes, but now I can't seem to get a certain blonde out of my head," Ronan rumbled and rolled his sleeves back. He had tattoos of intertwining tribal lines that disappeared under his shirt. How could arms make her mouth water? She leaned against the wall with her hands behind her back as she fought the urge to rip his shirt from his body. She wanted to discover how much was covered with ink, and then trace them with her tongue.

She imagined exploring every hill and valley of his arms and chest. She was picturing how he looked shirtless in his low-slung jeans when he moved and caught her attention. She looked up and noticed that he was staring at her expectantly. She chided herself at the lascivious bent of her thoughts. "The feeling is mutual. A certain bear shifter has been occupying my thoughts. What do we do about that?" She wanted to give in to her desire and get him out of her system. After all, he wanted to get back together with Claire, so there was no danger of a relationship.

He stalked around the desk and she retreated as he

neared her. Once he had her cornered, he grabbed her arm, sending a rush of electricity zinging across her skin. She marveled how the sensation went right to her core. Touching his skin was, simply put, euphoric. More than anything, she wanted to lean into him and wrap her arms around his neck before ravaging his mouth. She gazed up at him, willing him to make the first move.

"You couldn't handle what I have in mind," he drawled in that voice that had her abdomen clenching in need. Yes, she wanted to scream, she was ready...beyond ready. One touch would tell him just how ready she was.

"I'm pretty sure I can handle anything you can dish out." She knew it was a bold statement, and she was playing with fire, but she wanted to burn.

His glowing eyes traveled up and down every inch of her, arousing her further. "Then you'd better prepare yourself, little witch because I'm very hungry." Yes! She admitted to herself that she was more than happy to be incinerated by this magnificent male.

His eyes glowed cognac with his desire for her, yet he looked as if he hadn't wanted to say that. Not that it diminished her lust. She should be frightened that her need for him had only escalated. Her mind warned her of danger, but her body wasn't listening. She didn't even bother trying to get them on the same page, but let her body lead the way, reassuring herself that he didn't want a relationship with her.

He had come to them asking for a way to win Claire's heart back. It would be smokin' hot sex between them, nothing serious. Nothing serious was what she did, and she wanted this more than was good for her.

Her reasoning took that moment to return, and she panicked. He couldn't be a one-time kind of guy, given that he had been with someone for two hundred years. She refused to get involved in a relationship of any kind. She wanted him, but...

"I can see the wheels turning in that pretty little head of yours. Don't overthink this. Kiss me." He interrupted her internal debate and caressed her cheek, sending shivers down her spine.

"I'm not over thinking this. It's just that I'm seeing someone," she lied as she looked up into his handsome face. His eyes flashed to black with his anger and he grabbed her by the arms. She was in trouble now...the kind of trouble she loved.

CHAPTER 3

Ronan felt like a volcano ready to erupt, but he didn't give a shit at the moment. If he were being honest with himself, he hadn't been in control from the moment he had walked into the store hours ago. For some reason, Pema made all of his senses fire into overdrive, which drove him mad. He had been heading home with no intention of returning to the store, yet here he was, in the backroom alone with her, asking for a kiss and hoping for more.

His plan for weeks had been to find a way to win Claire back, and now he was insane with jealousy over Pema. At the moment, Claire was a distant memory.

The thought of Pema bedding another male made his mind snap. Not going to fucking happen. She was his to pleasure, and he needed to show her what no one else was capable of giving her. He tried to rein in his ardor, but rational thought was beyond him. He roughly shoved her against the wall and growled at her, his grizzly wanting to sink his teeth into the delicate skin of her neck and hold her in place while he took her body. He was too caught up in the moment to be disturbed by the fact that his grizzly had never wanted to be involved with Claire, the only woman he had ever loved.

He paused scant millimeters from her mouth and took her panting breaths as his own. "Liar," he accused, closing the gap.

She moaned and mumbled, "You caught me, there's no one else." He smiled and claimed her mouth for the first time.

Her lips were soft and succulent and tasted of ripe strawberries. Ronan had never felt anything like her drugging kiss. A growl worked its way up his throat. He was going to have her, and nothing else mattered. He wanted her mindless and writhing against him from the passion *he* invoked.

He licked and nipped at her until she parted her lips for him. When she opened her mouth, he took full advantage, delving deep. An electrical spark zapped his tongue when it touched hers, making his cock hard as stone. He had never really cared for kissing, not wanting the intimacy, and in fact, had rarely indulged with Claire. What a fool he had been, but then, it had certainly never felt like this for him.

His mind blanked as his lust took the wheel. He grabbed a handful of her hair and pulled her head back, more roughly than he intended, but by her sounds of pleasure and the scent of her arousal, she didn't mind. She was no wilting flower, and he almost came in his pants when she tried to climb his body. He loved how aggressive she was.

He gave into the sensations, praying she made him climax a hundred times. He thanked the Goddess that he was a powerful ursine shifter and had little to no refractory period, which meant he could go all fucking night if she'd let him. His free hand snaked down her side, his thumb brushing the outer curve of her breast.

He needed to feel her skin before he went insane, and slid a hand under the edge of her top. She was soft as rose petals and he almost fell on her like the raving beast he was. He wanted to shout his triumph as she lifted her leg and wrapped it around his hip. The action brought his hard and erect shaft in direct contact with her molten core and she muttered, "Someone's peeking out, wanting to play. Mmmm, I like it." He glanced down and saw that his rampant cock had snuck past the waist band of his jeans. They definitely had too many clothes on.

"Then you're gonna love what's next," he replied, claiming her mouth once again.

He luxuriated in the feel of her soft skin as his hand roamed up her soft belly to her breasts, their lips never parting. Finally, he had one of her breasts gripped in his hand, her pert nipple pressing through the silk of her bra into his palm. She was so responsive, grinding against him, moaning and grabbing at his shirt. Quick as a flash, she had the material over his head.

He pushed her hands away when she went for his pants next. He planned to explore her fully, and if she managed to get him naked, he wouldn't be able to stop. "Not right now, love. I am going to devour you first. I'm a bear, baby, and I need your honey."

"Oh, Goddess in *Annwyn*. We shouldn't…but, damn," she mumbled against his mouth.

"We're not going to think right now, just feel. Let me fuck you," he demanded. He had to sink into her tight, hot little sheath or surely he would go up in flames. He was too far gone, and thankfully, so was she.

"Sex. Just sex," she mumbled against his lips. Her words caused an ache in his chest. He briefly wondered if the ache was caused by unquenched desire, disappointment, or the fact that he was going to have sex with someone other than Claire. He had spent four hundred years living as a bear before she found him and coaxed him back to his human form. Claire was the only female he'd ever had sex with, but when Pema bit his ear and kissed her way to his neck, his thoughts dissolved in the blink of an eye.

He let go of her hair and had her shirt over her head before she took another breath. He took a moment to appreciate the sight of her breasts swelling with her desire against the scant fabric. Her nipples were pearled like the ripe berries he used to find in the woods, and damn, did he love those berries.

He leaned down and sucked a nipple into his mouth, biting it through the cloth. He relished her cry of pleasure. He pulled back and the sight of the wet fabric and straining flesh had him hardening more than he thought possible.

Ronan turned her around and pushed her up against the wall, reveling in her gasp as he unhinged her bra. She needed to know from the start who was in charge. She dropped her arms and the silk dropped to the floor. She glanced back at him over her shoulder and he nearly died at the look on her face. Her eyes were glazed with her desire and her lips were red and swollen from his kisses. If he had his way, she would always look like this.

"Put your hands on the wall and don't move them," he ordered. She gave him the sexiest smile he had ever seen, full of promise and intrigue.

"Yes, sir," she sassed. He swatted her magnificent ass, eliciting a moan. He knew that if he kept that up, she'd orgasm from his spanking alone.

"You like that," he murmured close to her ear, swatting her ass again. She moaned in response and he chuckled at her fervent nodding. Being with her was so natural that is scared him for a moment. The questions and concerns that bubbled up were quickly forgotten as she rubbed her ass against his groin.

Ronan growled and leaned his full weight against her back, kissing her neck and biting her ear lobe, reaching around to the front of her skinny jeans while he did. The button gave way and he had the zipper down before he gave in and tore the material from her body.

He kissed his way down her spine, loving how she squirmed and complained about him teasing her too much. He stood when her pants were pooled on the floor next to them and cupped her backside, giving it a firm squeeze. "This sweet ass is mine." He wasn't sure where the declaration came from, but had no desire to take the words back.

She twisted around and stood on tiptoe. "My ass belongs to no one," she breathed against his ear. He felt her bite down where his shoulder met his neck and then lick the sting. So damn good. He'd never had shivers from sexual play, but hell if they didn't travel throughout his body at that moment.

He pulled her flush against his body. He groaned at the feel of her moist feminine flesh touching the head of his shaft where it had escaped its confines. It almost brought him to his knees. It was better than he'd ever thought possible with so little contact.

He was both excited and full of trepidation at the thought of actually having sex with her. He hoped he didn't embarrass himself and lose his seed at the first stroke. "Your body tells a different story, little witch."

He rotated his hips and swallowed her gasp. "How would you know?" she moaned against his mouth, "You haven't learned the language my body speaks."

He wrapped one arm under her pert backside, holding

her up while he slid the fingers of his free hand between their bodies. He easily found her little bundle of nerves. It throbbed, begging him for attention. He pinched and teased her clit and soon she was riding his hand with abandon. He watched as her head thrashed from side to side, sending her long, blonde curls dancing across his naked chest and arms.

"I was wrong," she panted. "Holy shit...I've never been happier to be wrong." His fingers paused at her entrance, the heat scalding him. He slowly sank one finger in, then another and pressed his thumb against her clit. She went wild, bucking and rubbing against him. Her muscles clamped down on his fingers, she was close.

"Mine," he growled, shock widening his eyes. He had no idea where the assertion came from, him or his bear. If he didn't get inside her soon he would go insane. He withdrew his fingers from her and put them to his mouth. Her taste was like ambrosia.

"Can't," she muttered shaking her head. "Want you so much...shouldn't do this...don't stop."

Stop? He'd never stop. "Pema," he said her name, a promise and entreaty.

She placed her hands on his chest, digging her nails in while pushing against him, pushing him away. "We have to stop...this is too much." She was stopping now? When she was so close? He was barely coherent and didn't want to stop. That fact frightened him because, after all, he wanted to win Claire back. Right?

She took several deep breaths, causing her pearled nipples to brush against his skin. He closed his eyes, gathering his patience. He was going to die from unspent lust. After several silent moments, he opened his eyes and looked into her glazed sea-green eyes.

"Shit...you're right," he panted, gathering what wits he

could and pulling his shirt back on. He held her gaze for what seemed an eternity, waiting for her to say something, before he forced himself to leave.

∽

Cele watched her daughter pace her kitchen, arms flailing as she ranted. "I can't believe Ronan was pining over a Rowan. Kenny told me he overheard Ronan talking about her with Killian. He said it was more than obvious that he was interested in Pema. Why was it so important for me to end my relationship with him? I told you I loved him, and now weeks later, he has forgotten about me and moved on with a Rowan!"

Cele was stunned by her daughter's statements. She had taught her better. A Wells never allowed herself to become this distraught over a male. Males were to be used for pleasure and discarded, never kept and never fought over. Not to mention that the male her daughter coveted was a puny shifter. Males should be chosen for their power and what one could garner from them. Cele didn't regret that she had forced her daughter to end the relationship with Ronan. This little display of Claire's proved that it had gone too far.

Cele had chosen Claire's father with great care from a selection of the most powerful witches. When Cele had taken the High Priestess position, she had used dark magic to learn of her Fated Mate. When she discovered he was a weak shifter, she had been forced to eliminate him. It took Cele centuries and the use of that same dark magic to become pregnant with Claire. She had hand-selected a powerful witch to be the father.

Cele had hoped to bear the prophesized Adorned triplets. When that didn't happen, she became determined that her heir would be the most powerful witch in the realm, and she would do anything to ensure it. That was the reason she was going to force the prophesized Rowan triplets to cede their power to her.

Cele had been researching methods to siphon and utilize the triplets' power since their birth twenty-seven years ago and she was closer than ever. She needed all three witches alive for them to concede their magic to her. She already had a diamond pure enough to harness their power. With the power bound to the diamond, Cele would finally be able to take over the realm and subjugate that meddlesome council once and for all. She wasn't about to let Claire's infatuation interfere.

She would be unstoppable, and her daughter would take her place as High Priestess when she passed, ensuring her reign continued. In this, she wouldn't fail. She couldn't fail or she and her daughter would suffer the consequences. She recalled the oracle's prophecy to the High council hundreds of years ago.

When the earth devours the moon thrice, fate delivers her price. Those not meant to be carry three and the birth of the Adorned hold the key. Fate plus three power grew, malevolence demolished and balance found anew.

The enigmatic prophecy had troubled Cele, and she'd questioned the oracle after the meeting had ended. The hag had informed Cele that she was the malevolence that was going to be demolished. Enraged, Cele had told the oracle her prophecy about triplets being her downfall would never come to fruition...right before she slit her throat. She vowed then that nothing would stop her bid for power, and she wasn't about to give up now because her daughter wanted some flea-ridden animal.

"Mother, are you listening to me?" Claire demanded.

"I'm wondering why you are so upset over this male. You need to forget this weak bear and calm down. You are a Wells, start acting like one."

"I haven't lost my composure. I'm venting and planning the best ways to eliminate Pema, if you had been listening. I was asking how I should kill her," Claire huffed and placed her hands on her hips, the quintessential picture of outrage.

Oh, if it were only that easy, Cele thought bitterly. Claire had no idea the hornet's nest she was poking. Pema and her sisters had the power to bring harm to her daughter, and she needed to think fast to protect her baby girl.

"I told you to calm down," she barked and slid the pocket door to the kitchen closed. She needed to teach her daughter more discretion. There were too many ears about. "You cannot go around threatening these witches so openly."

She grabbed two wine glasses and opened a bottle of merlot, then guided Claire to a barstool. "This matter hardly warrants your attention. There are plenty of other males with whom you can amuse yourself. I understand you don't care for the triplets, but they are the key to our ruling the realm."

Claire accepted her glass of wine with a pout. "I don't want another male. I love Ronan and I miss being with him. I don't expect you to understand. Do you even remember what pleasure is? How long has it been?" Claire sneered.

Cele hated how immature her daughter was at times and wanted to strangle her. She was a centuries old witch, yet was sitting there obsessing about this situation, and it was driving Cele insane. Claire had always been like that though. She'd want something and whine about it until Cele used whatever means necessary to make sure she had it.

"Stop and think, daughter. Ronan doesn't matter in the grand scheme of life. Find another male and move on." Claire had better follow her advice or she'd regret it. The truth was Cele would kill Ronan before she allowed Claire to harm Pema. She needed the power of all three sisters combined, and having one of them dead defeated her purpose. Nothing, not even Claire, would interfere with her obtaining the power of three.

CHAPTER 4

Pema cursed her stupidity. She was aching and still humming from Ronan's touch. It had taken all of her willpower to push him away and put a stop to what had promised to be the best sex she'd ever had.

As close as she was to climaxing, calling a halt to their amorous play had been one of her dumber decisions. She had locked herself in place and refused to stop him when he had stomped out of the room. Remembering his sexy growls, hard, muscular chest and the sight of his long, thick shaft climbing out of his jeans wasn't helping her to calm down. She blanked her mind and took several deep breaths before she finally gathered her wits enough to exit the office.

It was a relief to escape the smell of his male musk and their combined arousal, which had only served to keep her on edge. Sure, she missed the male behind the scent and wanted him with a desperation that was unhealthy, but she refused to give into her desires. She had liked his claim on her way too much, and her mind had responded with a claim of its own. It made her question what was between them, so she had to stop him.

She didn't want a relationship. She never wanted to develop something that could be torn asunder. Watching her mother give in to her Fated Mate and crush her father's heart had torn their family apart. It devastated Pema to watch her father these past few months, and she had vowed that would never be her.

Everyone in the realm had been excited and was celebrating the return of Fated Mate blessings after seven long centuries. Everyone except her and her father. When Pema added her father's situation to the stories of how her grandmother had withered away within days of her grandfather's death, anything to do with mating was to be avoided in her book. Pema stalked down the hall, searching for her sisters. Being near them would balance her and bring back her reason.

She overheard Isis talking to Suvi. "I can't believe Pema got down and dirty with Claire's shifter. What the hell is she thinking?" Pema scowled at the conversation between her sisters. "This could cause a shit-storm of problems for us with Cele. Dammit, like we needed to give her another reason to target us!"

"Relax, sis. He is one hot piece-of-ass, is what she was thinking. I'm honestly surprised it didn't last longer. I'd have kept him in there for days, weeks, shit, for months. And, need I remind you, that Claire ended whatever she had with the shifter, so he isn't Claire's," Suvi sang out. Pema had reached the store front and saw Suvi was perched on the ladder where she was dusting the candles. Pema was momentarily distracted by the fact that Suvi was standing on a small wooden slat in six inch heels. The sight had disaster written all over it.

Then their words registered and she was irritated. She didn't need their criticism, she needed their calming presence. Far more upsetting and disturbing, was the fact that she didn't like the thought of anyone but her keeping Ronan anywhere for days. A strange ache bloomed in her chest. She didn't have time to evaluate that right now.

Her possessive feelings were far too dangerous and ridiculous. She had no right to stake a claim on him. Yes, he was a passionate male and had echoed her sentiments, but she saw the relief in his eyes when she called a halt to their sexcapade. The ache in her chest tightened. It wasn't disappointment, she told herself, trying to believe the lie.

All she could think about was the image of him heading to Claire and putting the erect cock he left with to use. The thought infuriated her. If that bear knew what was good for him, he wouldn't. The claim stormed into her brain that he was hers. She gritted her teeth and clenched her hands into fists. He was not her male, she had no claim on him and she never would. Pema's anger flared, and she knew the moment Isis had absorbed that anger because several glass jars exploded.

Pema and Suvi jumped, shielding their faces when the jars shattered and pieces flew in all directions. When the debris settled, Pema took several deep breaths, allowing her emotions to calm, chiding herself for losing control. She knew better than most how Isis absorbed negative energies from her and Suvi.

"You good?" she asked, glancing sideways at Isis, gauging her reaction. Isis stood rigid with her jaw and fists clenched tightly. After several moments, Isis spread her fingers, releasing her magic safely into the cement floor. This was one of the reasons they had installed the cement floor. It could absorb most energy without damage to their surroundings.

Pema recalled the time Callieach went up in flames.

Several of the other students had been making fun of Suvi's torn and patched jeans. Suvi was shouting angry spells at the group when Pema and Isis exited the building. Everything went haywire and a fire broke out. While the adults put out the flames, they sat apart from everyone else, enduring the frightened stares of the other children.

Frightened rumors spread about the three of them destroying the Academy. At ten years old, they hadn't understood exactly what had happened. It wasn't until similar episodes of lamps breaking and glass shattering each time Isis was angry about something that they realized it had been her. As young teens, they discovered that Isis absorbed their emotions when Pema was cornered by a boy in the stairwell of their apartment complex. Isis walked up as the boy was slinking away. She was unaware that Pema was furious about his unwanted advanced, but the overhead light had shattered.

A smile curved Pema's lips. Burning down Cele's training center had been the highlight of their brief stint with formal education. The memory was enough of a reminder for Pema to gain control. She wouldn't risk further damage to their hard-earned business. As it was, she hated that she had already been the cause of even minor damage. They would be expensive to replace and she couldn't think of a way to recoup any of the loss.

"Pema! First, you screw Claire's guy, and now you're making me blow up our tea jars. Those were imported from India, dammit," Isis snapped.

Pema took another deep breath at the mention of Ronan belonging to Claire and held it, not wanting to get worked up again. Claire ended whatever relationship she had with Ronan negating any claim she had to the sexy shifter. "I'll order new ones," she said through gritted teeth.

"But, right now, I need your help, preferably without the commentary."

Suvi chuckled and descended the ladder. Pema was shocked at how nimble her sister managed the steps in those shoes. It was truly impressive. "Yeah, we know what happened. I'm surprised you aren't still enjoying the forbidden fruit." Pema groaned at her sister's teasing. They were going to be relentless.

"Yeah," Isis laughed, leaning on their display case of moon-charged crystals. "What was the problem? Maybe his fruit was on the small side."

Their laughing and teasing ended abruptly and Pema figured her torment was written all over her face. Isis met her gaze then reached out and grabbed her hand. Suvi snagged Pema's other hand. Immediately, the tension lessened in her chest. This was exactly what she needed. The connection with her sister's finally broke through the sensual haze and crazy impulses, grounding her.

"He is hung like a horse and I wish I were in that room riding him instead of standing here with you two," Pema blew out a breath. "My head got twisted and I got spooked. Worst part, I didn't even get an orgasm out of it."

"What did that asshole do to you?" Isis spat out. She appreciated how her sisters came to her defense. They'd always had each other's backs and always would.

She looked up and smiled at her sister. "He didn't do anything I didn't encourage. It's more about this little voice in my head that wanted to claim him and I wasn't alone in that. I can't explain the feeling I had when he became all possessive of me, but it wasn't my usual revulsion. I've never felt that way before, and it was too much. You know that's not me." Love equaled heartbreak and loss, and she would never be a part of it.

Isis squeezed her fingers and Suvi grabbed Isis' free hand, completing their circle. Magic tingled from Pema's fingertips, up her arms, and flooded her entire body. The feeling of their joined magic was like a million tiny bubbles fizzing in her veins. Connected to her sisters, she could face any obstacle that came her way. "I can't believe my ears. You, wanting to claim someone?" Isis asked, shaking her head and sending her red hair flying.

"I've never understood why you were so opposed to a relationship," Suvi muttered at the same time. Pema glared at her youngest sister. At times, she lived in the clouds.

"How can you say that? Dad has barely left his house since mom left him. And you know how grandma just died after grandpa was killed. I don't ever want to put my heart on the line only to have it crushed so brutally later. No thanks, that's not for me," Pema responded.

At the mention of their parents, Pema was reminded of the fact that she wasn't on speaking terms with their mother. The reasons for their lack of communication caused Pema's heart to ache with sadness and bitterness.

Their parents, Keri Reinhart and Greg Rowan, were among the rarity in the realm. They weren't Fated Mates, which meant they weren't supposed to be able to have children together. When non-fated couples had children, they were called the Adorned, and by some miracle their parents had had triplets. Until recently, Pema thought her parents madly in love and inseparable. That all changed the moment their mom found her Fated Mate.

It was impossible for Pema to see their father so heartbroken, and not be enraged. She was shocked that her mother could betray her father like she had. Her mother had slept with another male, and in the span of a couple days Keri had not only cheated on Greg, she had left him, crushing the male she had loved for centuries.

Part of her wanted to reach out to her mother, but every time she thought about it, she became angry all over again. And, even contemplating it felt like a betrayal to her father. Pema rubbed at the ache in her chest and pushed the negative memories into a box, pulling herself back to the present.

"Just because they had bad experiences doesn't mean you will. You need to consider that mom wasn't wrong to make a life with her mate. It's the Goddess' will. You've never even stopped to ask mom what this has been like for her. Anyway, how can you resist a male who could scarcely take his eyes off of you?" Suvi asked. "I knew he'd come back for you. This isn't over between you and the bear. He will have you, and you will embrace your feelings before long."

Pema snatched her hand back as if it had been dipped in acid. Damn her sister. She had just declared that Pema would be with Ronan and embrace her feelings while the three of them were holding hands. She knew better than to make such a proclamation while they were united. Pema began to panic.

They weren't the hands of fate, but ever since she could remember, the power they wielded when physically connected to one another was as close as supernaturals came to the Goddess whose will determined fate. Pema didn't want to end up chasing after Ronan the rest of her life.

Refocusing on the matter at hand as dread settled in her stomach, Pema paced around the store. "I can't be with him. Not only do I refuse to be in a relationship, but I don't want to be connected to anything that might bring us to Cele's attention."

Isis' eyes flared brightly and the lights in the store flickered. "Goddess, I hate that female. She has always given me the creeps. With those beady eyes and tight bun, she reminds me of a rat. Ugh...I still swear the only reason she gave us the money for this shop was to have a way to control us after we refused to be brainwashed at her school. And her daughter is an imbecile. I'd like to kick both their asses."

"Isis, take it down a notch before more damage is done," Pema cautioned. "But, I agree. Cele does want to control us. It's one reason mom and dad didn't make us go back to the Academy. She overplayed her hand ranting and raving to mom and dad about the prophecy. Otherwise, I'm sure they would have kept us there."

"She's not very smart is she? She has underestimated us time and time again. I know she figured that we would spend so much time partying that we wouldn't be able to pay her loan back. The look of shock on her face when we paid the loan in full so quickly was priceless," Suvi said as she picked up stones from the RockCandy display.

Isis and Pema joined in and they continued to joke about Cele and Claire as they fell into their routine of rearranging displays. It took all of Pema's effort to remain engaged with her sisters when her mind continually drifted back to Ronan.

The shifter had power over her, and for the first time in her life, she was weak where a male was concerned. It was disgusting, really. Yet, if he walked in the room and crooked his finger at her, she would melt and follow.

She wanted to feel his lips on hers as he caressed her face. More than anything, she wanted to feel his hard length sink deep into her, assuaging the building ache. She sighed. Her obsession was becoming ridiculous. "I'm going to need your help staying away when I see him at the club opening. I don't want to throw myself at him and look like a fool,"

Pema told her sisters.

∼

Claire sat, fuming in the back of the club. Gossip had spread quickly about how Ronan had shown up at Confetti Too smelling of Pema. The Rowan sisters were always the talk of the realm, whether it was because they were the famed triplets, or because their sexual exploits usually involved the most powerful, or that they were sought after for their magic. She couldn't escape the inept witches and it was infuriating.

She had called Ronan several times, but he hadn't answered. She had come to the club seeking him to make amends and was disappointed when he wasn't at the doors. His truck was in the parking lot, so she knew he was around somewhere.

Nerves riding high, she stood up and headed to the back halls of the newly built Confetti Too, thinking maybe he was in the staff room getting ready for his shift. She planned to seduce him and remind him of what they had shared for so many years. Pema couldn't hold a candle to what Claire meant to him.

Her heart was racing in her chest as she stalked down the hall. She stopped outside the door marked office when she heard the unmistakable rumble of Ronan's voice. She pulled out a compact and checked her lipstick before straightening her clothing. Her hands were sweating as she reached out for the doorknob.

She stopped to wipe her hands on her skirt and considered the best tactic for getting him back. Her mother had made it clear she wouldn't tolerate Claire being with Ronan, that he was beneath Claire. She didn't care what her mother said. She had never been the dutiful daughter and wasn't about to start following her mother's orders now.

Doubt about his feelings for her surfaced and she knew she needed to be sure she was going to have his full attention. She refused to have any of his thoughts linger on Pema and would do anything to ensure they didn't. Good thing she had planned ahead, she thought, as she pulled out a small vial from her purse and swished the clear liquid. It stung to resort to a love potion to retain his attention, but desperate situations called for desperate measures.

Crossing the hall, she hid from the open doorway and rested her sweaty palms on the wall behind her. There was no telling how angry he'd be if he saw her lurking outside the door. Nerves wracked her and Ronan's raised voice had her holding her breath. He was upset about something and having a heated discussion with someone.

"I'm sorry I stormed out on you today. Things got out of control and they shouldn't have. You were right to stop things from going further. Honestly, I don't have a clue what came over me. I hadn't intended for that to happen when I returned. I'm not even certain why I did come back, but it wasn't for that."

Claire's heart dropped to her feet at hearing Ronan's words. She wondered if he was talking to Pema, and if so, what did he mean by stopping things? Did that mean he hadn't had sex with her?

Ronan's voice interrupted her musings. "No, Pema, I can't deny the connection between us and I can't stop thinking about you."

Her heart twisted in her chest at the confirmation he was talking to Pema and she couldn't believe her ears. When did he develop this connection to Pema? He'd never told her that in all the years they had been together. For that matter, the tone of his voice had never been so soft and caring. What was it about Pema that had him giving her so much?

Claire struggled to hold her temper and not storm in the room, forcing the love-potion down his throat. No matter what it took, Ronan would be hers again.

"I don't want that either," Ronan suddenly growled.

Despite her mother's warning, she was going to take matters into her own hands. No one was coming between her and her male, especially not a Rowan.

CHAPTER 5

Pema looked around the new realm club as she stood with her sisters and the Dark Warriors at one of the larger tables. Killian had done a fantastic job with the new place. She was glad to see that he had managed to salvage the glass blocks he'd had in the original club, although, it was now topped with a sleek sheet of live-edged wood. The small, colored lights that were built into the glass blocks were twinkling on the legs of patrons sitting on the high-backed stools at the bar.

She noted there were natural elements everywhere in the club. Killian's shift away from the industrial décor in the original club gave the new place a feeling of warmth that had been lacking before.

Being a witch, she was connected to everything of the earth and felt grounded here. She surmised that Killian had made the change to enhance the protection she and her sisters had woven into the walls. They had been honored when Kill had asked them to add their own spells to those he and fellow sorcerers had already implemented. The club was all but impenetrable, and anyone, including the archdemons, would be hard-pressed to break their barrier.

"Nice skirt, witch. It'd look even better on my bedroom floor," a fire demon called out from the next table. Her head turned and she saw that the male's flame-orange gaze was trained on her ass.

"Keep your paws to yourself, this material isn't flame retardant," Pema called back then glanced down at her outfit, thinking she had gone overboard.

Self-loathing warred with common sense in her mind. She had dressed to provoke Ronan. Dressing for one specific male was completely out of her character and she hated that she had done it for Ronan. No, her inner-pep-talk chimed in, she was known for her risqué attire, and this had nothing to do with the bear. She was going with that thought. She had dressed for herself and no one else. She wondered if this was an omen that she was going to be lying to herself from here on out.

Try as she might, she wasn't able to stop from thinking about how it had pissed her off when he'd said he didn't want a relationship with her either. It didn't matter that she didn't want more from him. But then, she mused, it was always that way. When one person didn't want you, it made you want them even more. And what she wanted from him was dark and dirty. Her rampant hormones had been torturing her from the moment she had refused sex with the shifter.

But right now, what she wanted was for him to eat his words, and her clothing was meant to entice. It was clearly doing its job as the fire demon continued to try and cajole her.

She heaved a deep sigh, thinking panties would have been a wise choice tonight. Especially, given the ultra-miniskirt she was wearing. Maybe a bra too, although the bandeau top was restrictive enough that it didn't make that point too obvious. She would be fine as long as she didn't catch Ronan's scent. If she did, there would be no hiding her need.

She cursed silently when she realized her sisters had abandoned her at the table. She looked around the bustling club and saw that Suvi was with Bhric and heading to one of the backrooms. That was fast, she mused, as she shook her head. In fact, it had to be a record, even for Suvi. But, her sister did have a penchant for vampires, and the sexy Vampire Prince was always happy to oblige. That was one of the reasons Suvi had named her familiar, a black bat, after the Prince.

She spotted Isis on the dance floor with Rhys, one of the Dark Warriors. Pema smiled at the cambion's version of dancing, which involved a lot of bumping and grinding and tongue action.

Male posturing brought her back to her immediate surroundings. Gerrick, another the Dark Warriors, was about to throw down with the fire demon that had been hitting on her. From the words being exchanged, Gerrick had taken up for her when she had become distracted. Being welcomed into the Vampire King's close ring of friends was new to them and she found she really liked the formidable males. They were surprisingly down-to-earth.

When Gerrick grabbed the demon by the scruff of the neck and led him away, she noticed Ronan had responded to the raised voices and was heading in their direction, looking as delicious as ever. Searching for a distraction from her desire to get up and run into Ronan's arms, she turned to Cailyn and Jace who were sitting to the side of her.

A few weeks ago, Pema and her sisters had helped Jace, a

Dark Warrior discover a spell that had been buried deep inside his psyche for over seven centuries. It was what had brought them into Zander's inner circle.

"We haven't had a chance to follow up and see if you were able to break Angelica's spell," Pema said to Jace, trying not to breathe through her nose. It was bad enough she could hear Ronan's heavy footsteps and the deep rumble of his voice. She didn't need to add his luscious scent to the volatile mix churning in her gut.

Jace looked at her, his gratitude clear in his amethyst eyes. "It wasn't easy, but yes, with the love of my mate the spell was broken. I cannot fathom what my life would be like if you and your sisters hadn't revealed it. We owe you more than what we paid you. There is no reward big enough for the life you and your sisters made possible."

"Jace is right, we will never be able to repay you, but if you ever need anything, all you have to do is call. You're one of us now. Your sisters too," Cailyn declared. She was a delicate human female. Well, not so human anymore. They had completed their mating and Pema sensed the shift in the female's DNA that indicated she was now immortal like her mate.

"You owe us nothing. It was an honor to be called upon for such an important task. Not many in the realm would have taken the chance on us. We are impetuous, untrained witches," Pema teased and winked at Cailyn. "Seriously though, I'm glad that we were able to help. And, it was the most challenging spell we have ever cast, so we actually owe you. Because we didn't attend Callieach, we are never given the opportunity to practice such magic. Many of our customers are humans, only interested in love potions and tarot readings," she laughed.

Black Moon's top seller was their temporary love spells,

which were lust potions really. To sell actual love potions would take free will away from an unsuspecting being, something they would never do. Speaking of lust, her body suddenly ignited with it. Her stomach clenched with need as her feminine folds heated and moistened. She drew in a breath, Goddess, Ronan was near.

Pema surreptitiously glanced around the bar as she listened to Jace and Cailyn. Her heart sank when she saw Ronan waylaid by Claire, wearing a skin-tight, red dress with come-fuck-me heels. She couldn't be more desperate, Pema thought disdainfully, ignoring the hypocrisy of her own six inch stilettos.

Had he gone to her when he left Pema and rekindled their relationship? The thought made Pema flare her fingers, wanting to scratch her eyes out. She had broken things off with Ronan, yet now she was rubbing against him like a dog in heat.

Unable to tear her focus from Ronan, Pema ate him up with her eyes. Damn, he looked good in his low-ride, dark, denim jeans. His powerful thighs enhanced the bulge she could see growing in his pants. His tight, powder blue t-shirt molded to his broad shoulders and muscular pecs and set off his curly brown hair and dark, chocolate eyes. He was totally lickable. One curl hung adorably over his left eye and Pema all but drooled on the table in front of her.

Pema had to ignore the fact that Claire was clinging to his arm like fungus. It was either that or give into her violent urges. And didn't that set off an epic battle in Pema's mind. She wanted to stake a claim on Ronan so Claire and any other female knew just who he belonged to. Yet, she didn't want a relationship with him, or anyone else, for that matter. She saw the irony in that, but couldn't help it.

Part of her, she realized, had already staked a claim on

Ronan because when Claire pressed her body along Ronan's side and reached to pull him down to her waiting lips, Pema bared her teeth and hissed at the sight. She was mortified, she had never hissed at anyone before in her life.

"You okay, sweet cheeks?" Rhys asked, stepping into Pema's line of vision. She had been so consumed by Ronan and Claire that she hadn't seen him approach her. Never mind that she had completely checked out of her conversation with Jace and Cailyn.

"I can smell your arousal...and anger," Rhys purred. "I can help with that."

Heat flooded her cheeks with embarrassment and Rhys smiled that smile of his that usually had her grabbing at his jeans. Lamentably, her body desired only Ronan at the moment. It had to be because she had denied her body the sexy bear shifter and it wanted that experience. She refused to believe anything else.

"Fucking Rhys," she smiled up at him and winked, allowing him to wrap her in his arms. She knew she was being petulant by hoping to gain Ronan's attention with the cambion's embrace. It was nearly too much for her when Rhys grabbed her ass and pulled her against his groin. She became dizzy as her chest constricted painfully. She immediately became alarmed at the chest pain, wondering what had caused it. She prayed it was indigestion because the alternative didn't warrant consideration.

From the corner of her eye, she noticed that Ronan had stepped away from Claire and was staring at her. Pema's flash of satisfaction quickly died when Ronan's eyes turned to coal with his anger. Killian would fire him if he started a fight, especially when it was his job to stop such altercations. And she worried for his safety if he fought Rhys. Not that Ronan was weak, but Rhys was a powerful Dark Warrior.

She wasn't sure which of them would win a fight, but didn't want to find out.

When Ronan started forward, only to be pulled back by Claire, Pema's good sense flew out the window. Her muscles tensed and she was about to leap when Rhys stopped her dead in her tracks.

Ronan's nostrils flared and she had no doubt he could smell her arousal. The petty side of her was glad, because maybe seeing her with another male tortured him as much as the sight of him with Claire tortured her. Satisfaction wasn't as sweet as she thought it would be when she saw hurt cross his expression. Claire's satisfied smirk and possessive hold on Ronan had Pema's anger boiling right back to the surface. In an instant, Pema was poised and ready to attack.

"Stop, sweet cheeks. You don't want to do what you're thinking," Rhys whispered against her ear. How he had known, she wasn't certain, but he was right, attacking Claire would be a mistake. Pema closed her eyes and took a deep breath. The witch wasn't worth the effort.

Pema opened her eyes and enjoyed it far too much when Ronan walked away, leaving Claire alone at the bar. She dropped her head onto Rhys' shoulder as relief swamped her. She needed a drink, or ten, if she was going to make it through the night. "You're right, thank you, Rhys. I *really* need a vodka tonic."

"I got it, sweetness, something to occupy your mind and numb your body." Rhys teased as he sauntered up to the bar to order drinks.

CHAPTER 6

"I see the Dark Warriors are slumming with the Rowans," Claire told Rhys when he walked up to the bar. Pema clenched her jaw as she overheard Claire's haughty voice. It was like fingernails on a chalkboard and made her skin crawl. Ronan was only a recent addition to a long-standing list of reasons she hated the female. Pema didn't catch Rhys' response to Claire because she was busy fantasizing of ways to maim and kill Claire.

The sight of Ronan approaching a table where the patrons were involved in a heated argument distracted her. The way he wrapped his thickly muscled arm around one male's neck effectively delivered his threat and the table immediately settled. He prowled throughout the club keeping the patrons in check with his presence, and Pema enjoyed the view of his backside.

The sound of ice tinkling in a glass interrupted her ogling. A drink appeared in front of her, but it didn't look like what she had ordered. "That's not a vodka tonic, Rhys." She raised an eyebrow in question to the sexy warrior.

Rhys chuckled and wrapped his arms around her waist.

"No, it's not. I ordered you a screaming orgasm…a prelude of what's to come." The warrior waggled his eyebrows suggestively.

She laughed at him and shook her head. Over the noise in the club, Pema was able to hear Ronan's deep timbre as he spoke to various patrons. That voice did things to her that she both hated and loved, arousing her to an unbearable level. She needed that drink, now. "You know I'm not that easy," she replied to Rhys and downed the concoction in one swallow. "About that vodka tonic…"

"Anything the lady wants, but, I can help ease that tension much better than alcohol," Rhys said and pulled a glass from behind his back, handing it to her. Pema would have replied if she wasn't too busy covertly watching Ronan.

She wanted to go to Ronan and take him back to one of the rooms and finish what they had started. Pema stepped back into Rhys, fighting with all her might against her desires for Ronan. As if sensing her dilemma, Isis closed ranks on her other side and grabbed her hand, silently giving her support.

She and Isis both gritted their teeth as she watched Claire approach Ronan and engage in a conversation. She wanted to hear what they were saying and it was killing her that she couldn't. Why was he nodding to Claire? What was he telling her? Had they gotten back together? Insecurities and doubt, emotions Pema wasn't familiar with, swamped her as she wondered what he was thinking.

"Did you hear what I said, Pema?" Jace queried, looking at her with amusement.

As Pema turned her attention back to the table, she cursed herself for once again ignoring what was going on around her. She wished she wasn't so preoccupied. What made it worse was that if her body had its way, her world would narrow down to Ronan. She needed to pull her head out of her ass, like yesterday. "Sorry, I'm a bit distracted tonight. What were you saying?"

"I was explaining why Rhys can't go home with you and your sisters," Jace said with a laugh, enfolding his mate in his arms. The sight of them made her chest ache. She wondered what was happening to her. She didn't get gooey-eyed or mushy over couples and hardly recognized herself.

"We can't afford to lose him at the compound for the next month. With Kadir upping his game, we need all the Dark Warriors right now," Jace continued.

Pema and her sisters had remained on the outskirts of the battle between the Dark Warriors and the archdemons and their skirm. But, they hadn't agreed with Cele's declaration that it wasn't the witches' problem. Pema felt the witches could make a difference in winning the war if they joined their powers to the Dark Alliance council and added witches to the Dark Warrior ranks.

Before she lost focus again, she responded to Jace. "I imagine that with you and Zander now mated, life at the compound is different. Nightly patrols are likely at the bottom of the list of things you'd rather be doing. Is Thane going to be relocated here?" Pema asked as she saw Cailyn's friend, Jessie, leaving the dance floor with the San Francisco Dark Warrior.

"I'm not sure, but I think Jessie would like that," Cailyn laughed.

Pema smiled at that. Yes, she believed Jessie would. "Hey, Dhampir, how's it going? Eat any people recently?" Pema asked Jessie.

"Hey, witch," Jessie said, giving her a high-five. "I'm good, and no, I haven't eaten any people. I prefer Dark

Warriors," she said and snapped her teeth at Thane, who swatted her behind playfully.

"I can see that. Me, I'm learning I have a sudden urge for shifters," Pema retorted. Someone bumped into her shoulder, causing her to teeter on her heels. She regained her balance and looked to the side to see that it had been Claire. Petty, Pema thought, as the jostled glasses clinked on the table.

"Excuse you," Pema said through gritted teeth. When Claire ignored her, she called out loudly, "Enjoy your evening!"

Claire changed direction and sauntered up to Ronan where he stood by the front door. "Take a break and let's go to one of Kill's back rooms," Claire said loud enough for Pema to hear. Isis grabbed Pema's hand and took her attention from the couple. She downed her drink, grimacing at the bitter after-taste, wondering what Rhys had ordered her this time.

"Come on, let's dance," Pema said, grabbing Rhys' hand and tugging Isis with them.

"Alright, sweet cheeks. Or we could skip the dance," Rhys wheedled.

"We're going to dance, Romeo," she insisted.

"I'm going to change your mind, Pema," Rhys tried again. She swatted his arm and smiled at her sister, grateful to have her at her side. The bond she shared with both her sisters was a lifeline that she prayed would pull her through whatever had possessed her at the moment.

Forgetting her troubles for the time being, Pema grabbed Isis and began an erotic dance with the two of them caging Rhys. The bass and beat vibrated through her and thumped in her veins. Typically, she lost herself in the rhythm of music, but she was continuously looking over to see if Ronan was watching. She noticed he was and that his eyes blazed with a range of emotions she couldn't identify.

The connection she felt to Ronan throbbed with their shared desire. He wanted her as much as she wanted him, and that made the prospect of being with him that much more dangerous. Pema threw herself into the dance as a distraction from her urge to fuck him senseless.

Without warning, Pema began to sweat and her heart started racing. She slowed her movements, trying to calm down. Fatigue slammed into her and she could barely stay upright. It frightened her when her arms turned to lead and her vision went fuzzy. Being a supernatural, she wasn't prone to illness so she had no idea what was wrong. She swayed under the onslaught.

Suddenly, she doubled over as pain ravaged her stomach and she lost her breath. This was no illness. Something teased the edges of her mind, something about her drink. Forming a coherent thought was currently beyond her ability. Her sister and Rhys had both stopped dancing and their blurred faces were in her line of vision.

She heard her sister speaking to her but was unable to respond through the dizziness. She was going down. How embarrassing for everyone to see this, especially Ronan. She needed to tell them something…but what…the bitter aftertaste! Strong arms caught her as the cement floor rushed to greet her.

She gazed up into Rhys' kaleidoscope eyes. "What is it, Pema? You don't look so good. Do you know what's wrong?"

"Drink…" she struggled to talk, and coughed, tasting blood. "Poison…" she mumbled, barely audible due to the swelling in her throat. She shut her eyes and focused on trying to take a breath. She needed to slow the progress of whatever was pumping through her system. Her attempt to mutter a stasis spell came out jumbled.

The world swam when she opened her eyes. Everything was blurry and her stomach revolted. Rhys picked her up and was hurrying off the dance floor, shouting, "Jace, something is wrong with Pema! Get your ass over here! She mentioned something about poison!"

"Set her down on the table," Jace's voice sounded closer than she expected. It was comforting to hear how calm and collected he was. She knew she was in bad shape and was grateful that the healer was at the club. If anyone could fix her, it was Jace.

"Pema, can you hear me? It's Jace." She tried to open her mouth and talk, but nothing worked. She nodded her head or thought she did, it was difficult to tell. "I'm going to put my hands on your stomach. You will feel warmth as I heal you. Stay with me, I need you to talk to me, tell me why you think it was poison. What did you taste? Rhys, grab an unopened bottle of water. Kill, grab a cold cloth." Jace talked to her and issued orders without missing a beat and she felt hands land on her bare abdomen.

A wonderful, warming sensation began in her belly and spread out from there. Her heart stuttered then stopped, before it continued racing. The swelling was thankfully going down in her throat and she sucked in a breath. "Drink...tasted bitter," she whispered.

"We can smell it now. Don't worry, just drink this," Jace instructed as he helped her sit up slightly with a hand behind her shoulders.

"Pema!" Ronan roared from somewhere across the room. She cracked her eyes open and saw Ronan rush towards her with panic in his eyes. Behind him, she saw Claire being drug from the bar. Was that Cele taking Claire away? Yes,

Pema would know that tight bun and stiff spine anywhere. She had no doubt that they were responsible. Glass shattered on the tables around her, causing people to shriek. Through her haze she saw that Isis was pissed. For once, she hoped Isis unleashed hell on the High Priestess and her daughter.

∽

RONAN PUSHED his way to Pema's side. He had no idea what had happened, only that Pema was injured. The triumphant gleam in Claire's eyes as her mother pulled her from the club told him that Claire was responsible. He cursed himself for being so preoccupied with his turbulent emotions.

No matter how much he had wanted to repair his relationship with Claire, he hadn't been able to shake his desire for Pema. The moment he saw Pema walk in the club, his jaw had dropped open. She looked sexy as hell and every male eye in the place had been on her. Claire couldn't have been more obvious with her jealousy of Pema.

As he ate up the distance, rage made him see red that Claire had harmed an innocent. He had spent two centuries with her and would never have guessed that she was capable of such treachery. His anger quickly turned inwards that on his first night on the job, he'd failed. He was responsible for the safety of patrons in the club. Yet, Pema had been injured under his watch.

When he crouched next to Pema and grabbed her limp hand, the scent of poison hit him with her every exhalation. "I'm so sorry that this happened. I failed you. I promise nothing like this will ever happen again." Pema didn't respond, only closed her eyes as Jace continued his work.

Losing Pema was unacceptable. He had no idea how or

why or when this female had gotten so deep under his skin, but she had. The thought scared the shit out of him. The fact that Claire had done this was even scarier. He'd never forget the triumphant expression on her face as she left the club. It was the most chilling sight he'd ever seen.

Thoughts of Claire had him leashing his bear as anger at her actions tore through him. Up until this point, if anyone had asked him, he'd have told them Claire wasn't capable of harming a fly. His stomach flipped as his world was thrown in a blender on high speed.

He may have wanted to win Claire back, but the truth was, this act was unforgivable and he would never be able to look at her the same again. In that one second, Ronan questioned everything he had ever known or believed.

He bent to kiss Pema's forehead. "You're going to be the death of me. What am I going to do with you?" he murmured in her ear.

CHAPTER 7

Ronan gazed into pained sea-green eyes and his heart broke for what the female was suffering. The death of his family destroyed any softer emotion he'd ever felt, but this witch brought out a side of him he hadn't believed possible. Sure, he had loved Claire, but this was something altogether different. It was tender, passionate, full of heat, and raw lust. It left him breathless and exhilarated, and he wasn't exactly comfortable with it. He had no frame of reference or any idea how to deal with what was rolling through him.

Bringing his attention back to the matter at hand, he noticed that the music had stopped and the club goers were gawking at their group. He caught the tail end of the question Jace posed to Pema. "...would do this to you? What enemies do you have? It couldn't have been a Fae or one of Kadir's allies. Killian said none of the alarms were triggered."

"Everything is fine here. Let's get back to the fun, this is supposed to be a party," Killian announced and motioned to the DJ. The club-goers were slow to return to their activities, but once music blared through the speakers, they gradually edged away from the table.

Pema's hoarse voice had him itching to take her into his arms. "I don't have that many enemies. Not that it matters how many enemies I have...Claire and Cele did this. There is no doubt in my mind." Ronan had seen the look on Claire's face and agreed with Pema, Claire was responsible.

"I'm going to relish causing that bitch pain and agony before I rip her head from her shoulders," Isis snarled, causing the overhead lights to flicker. Magic, Ronan recognized with discomfort, recalling how Killian had choked him without even touching him. Claire had never performed real magic in his mind, and here they were displaying their power every time he turned around.

He recalled Killian's earlier warning regarding the danger Cele posed, and suddenly felt an overwhelming need to protect Pema. He made a mental note to ask Killian about ways to protect against spells. Surely, the sorcerer had some helpful information.

"No one is doing any killing," Rhys responded as he grabbed Isis' hand. "At least not right now. Come on, you can help me look for evidence to present to the elders."

"I want to nail her to the wall. I'll be back, Pema," Isis bent over and kissed Pema's forehead before turning to the Dark Warrior. "Rhys, grab the glass she drank out of," Isis ordered.

Seeing the severity of the situation more fully, Ronan reconsidered. Perhaps Claire hadn't done it. If she did, then she was in a world of trouble. Isis and Rhys clearly had Pema's back and would find any evidence necessary to prove Claire's guilt, and in their world, the trials were brief, and punishment for this crime was death. He felt like he should be defending the female he'd spent his life with and had loved for so long, but he knew deep-down in his gut she was guilty and he would never excuse what she had done.

He had been torn in a million different directions in the span of minutes. He'd never put any credence in the idea that fate had a hand in decisions, but he couldn't help questioning it. There were many fables in the realm about the Goddess and her power that he'd never considered. As he gazed down into beautiful sea-green eyes, he couldn't deny that he was meant to be in this city, with this enchanting witch.

Jace straightened, speaking to Pema, "You will likely be dizzy and nauseous for a bit yet. You need to go home and lie down."

"I'll take her to the bed in back," Ronan rushed to offer, "and make sure she gets some rest while they finish their investigation," ignoring the hundred different fantasies playing through his mind that involved anything but rest.

Ronan scooped Pema into his arms before anyone could object. Pressing her warm body against his, he inhaled her sweet strawberry scent...Goddess, it was addicting. Her curves fit perfectly against him, making lust course through him and harden his shaft.

He began heading to the rooms in back when Jace's voice had him turning back. "Make sure she drinks some more water, as well. I nullified the poison, but she needs to flush it from her system."

"Will do. And, thanks for saving her," Ronan replied and turned away after Jace nodded his acknowledgment.

"Where are you taking me?" Pema asked, looking up at him with huge doe-eyes. There was a storm brewing in her sea-green depths, and it electrified him.

"There is a room with a bed in back. I had thought

Killian crazy for including it, but right now I'm glad he did." He gently tucked a strand of hair behind her ear.

"I'm not sure being in a room alone with you and a bed is a good idea," Pema whispered with a small curve to her lips.

Ronan leaned his face down to hers until their lips were scant inches apart as he paused outside the door. "Afraid you won't be able to keep your hands off of me?" he asked as he twisted the knob and pushed the door open. He pressed his lips against hers lightly then crossed the threshold and kicked the door closed.

"It's not my hands I'm worried about," she countered and stretched her neck, seeking his lips once again. When their lips met with more force this time, he had to remind himself to be gentle, that she had just been poisoned.

"Good, I want them all over me. And, I want my tongue over every inch of your luscious body," he blurted before he could stop himself. She bit his lower lip and it took all of his considerable strength to pull back. "How are you feeling? Jace said you should rest and I need to get you some water."

She placed her hand on his chest. "I don't want to rest," she murmured, claiming his lips once again.

"Are you up for this? Be sure, because there will be no stopping this time." The words escaped him with a harsh growl.

She closed her eyes, a bevy of emotions playing across her features. After what seemed like an eternity she met his glowing gaze. "I feel fine and I want you. I want to have sex with you."

He turned her in his hold and relished when she wrapped her legs around his waist. He roughly ground his erection against her core. He glanced down and saw she wasn't wearing panties, so fucking sexy. "The best sex of your life." He grinned and dropped her onto the bed. With quick movements, he had her clothing in a pile on the floor.

He stared for long moments at her pale, creamy skin. She was breathtaking. He ran his fingers up her legs, skimming over her wet, needy core, eliciting moans that had his cock jerking in anticipation. Her breasts beckoned and he stopped to give them the attention they deserved. He rolled pert nipples between his thumb and forefinger then bent and sucked one into his mouth.

It was the easiest thing in the world to get lost in this female. As he licked and teased the most exquisite breasts he had ever seen, his hand traveled down the flat planes of her abdomen. He took a deep breath and reminded himself that she'd just been poisoned and he needed to be gentle. When her muscles quivered beneath his palm, it drove his control out the window. She was as desperate for him as he was for her.

He lifted his head and saw she had thrown her head back on the pillow. He dipped one finger into her slit and caressed her moist, feminine flesh. "So hot and wet, and, it's all for me," he whispered, licking his lips that were craving a taste of her.

"Yes, for you...please..." she trailed off, thrashing her head back and forth and lifting her hips seeking more from his touch. Anxious to see her lost to his ministrations, he sank one, then two, fingers into her core while his thumb found her clit.

He returned his mouth to her breasts and licked and nipped her flesh. She gasped his name and began riding his hand fervently. When she was close to orgasm, he pulled back and stilled his movements.

"You're killing me," she complained. "Make me come or fuck me now," she begged in an urgent tone.

"Not yet, I need your honey." She had no idea how desperate he was to lick and suck her sweet juices. His cock had a mind all its own, needing her cream to coat every inch of its length as he pounded her into the mattress.

Later, he promised himself, right now he was anxious for her cream to flow down his throat. He lifted his head and spread her legs wide while he knelt on the bed and lifted her bottom in his hands. The firm globes filled his palms. He playfully bit her silky ass before he leaned back, staring at her. She was fucking perfect.

Before he knew what was happening, she had quickly sat up and ripped his shirt off his body, throwing it to the floor. Oh, he liked how aggressive his female was. Wait, *his*? He shook his head even as he laughed out loud, he wasn't going there.

His mind may still be reeling from what had happened with Claire, but he had been obsessed with Pema for the past twenty-four hours and he needed her. Pema had almost died. He clasped her to him, relishing her racing heart as a reminder that she was alive. He had no idea what he was going to do about Claire, but he wasn't going to let that stop him from enjoying this moment with Pema. She was naked and beautiful and wanted him.

He slid his hands around her waist and laid his body over the top of hers. He groaned at the feel of his bare chest pressed against her front. Her legs fell open and she gave herself to him, trusting him with her body.

She ran her hands over his chest, gripping his pecs. "Mmmm, you feel so damn good. Your hair is silky-soft and making me crazy. Get inside me now!"

"No, love." He went to his knees again and knew this was how she deserved to have her male...on his knees, worshipping her perfection.

Her arousal perfumed the air around them. Patience was lost on him and he squeezed her ass. His bear was clamoring to claim her ass and show her that she was his. Not the thought he wanted at that moment, and he shook it off. The pent up lust from being denied yesterday was messing with his head. Time to remedy that.

"Oh, Ronan," she cried out.

He spread the flesh at the apex of her thighs and licked from her opening all the way to her nether hole where he teased her. She shuddered with pleasure. He knew then and there his bear wouldn't have to wait long.

He remembered stocking the room and jumped up and grabbed the jar of honey he had placed among the other implements. His co-workers had laughed at him for putting honey with the ball-gags and lubricant, but he had told them that many species liked treats added to their sexual play. He was glad he had followed instinct and left the jar there.

He stalked back to the bed and met her half-lidded eyes. He flipped the cap then drizzled it between her succulent folds before he sat down and positioned his body between her legs. Her arousal combined with the honey glistened in the dim, overhead lighting. He ran his finger through her slit, teasing her pulsing clit before tracing back to her core.

He fingered her pussy then continued further to tease her anus. "Do you shave, baby?" He had never had a female who was bare, but he loved having nothing in the way of sampling her arousal. Her scent called to him and he licked one long path from her core to her throbbing clit. She tasted of strawberries and honey, and now, he was ravenous.

"Goddess," she called out. "No, I don't shave. Witchcraft," she gasped. He loved how responsive she was to his touch. Her panting was music to his ears.

"You're able to think too clearly for my liking. I'm going to correct that. Close your eyes. Give yourself over to me." He felt like he had won the lottery when she obliged, spreading her legs further apart.

Like the wild animal he had deep inside, he devoured her moist, feminine folds. She cried out when he nipped and sucked her clit. She was mumbling incoherently from the onslaught of his tongue lashing her. He was unable to think of anything except bringing her pleasure then plunging deep inside her. She drove him mad and he loved it.

Pema was the most responsive female he had ever been with. Her skin was like lava beneath his fingertips where he gripped her buttocks. She writhed and shifted her hips in time to his ministrations. His cock was hard and begging to feel her tight, hot sheath, yet, it was surprisingly easy to ignore his own desire when he was pleasuring Pema.

He thrust his tongue into her channel and felt her muscles clamp down. She lifted her hips off the bed as she attempted to get more pressure and friction to her throbbing bundle of nerves.

More beast than man at the moment, Ronan replaced his tongue with two of his fingers and sucked her clit into his mouth. He flicked the nub with his tongue and increased suction while scissoring his fingers in and out of her body. She fisted the bedspread, her eyes snapped open and she detonated, coming in a rush. His name left her lips in a litany as the spasms racked her. He pulled his fingers free and stood up, tearing at the zipper of pants to free his shaft.

Pema attempted to help him, but he held her still with one hand. For an instant, his heart stopped. She had gone to her hands and knees. He managed to free himself and had his cock in hand, ready to thrust into the ass she had arched back to him and claim her fully. He barely held back the instinct. He had never before had the desire to claim Claire, or any female like that. For shifters, that was reserved for their Fated Mate. Could she be his?

Before he gave that question anymore consideration, Pema met his eyes over her shoulder, capturing his undivided attention. "Fuck me, Ronan. Forget the rest. Right now, I need your cock inside me."

"Brace your hands on the wall, baby. I can't hold back," he ordered as he pulled his hips back then thrust into her pussy in one stroke. He stilled the moment he was seated fully inside her body, allowing her to adjust to his length. Her muscles rippled around his shaft deliciously as her pussy gripped him like a fist.

"Ah, Goddess, Pema. You feel so good. I hope you want it hard and fast." He punctuated his words with a twist of his hips, making her cry out.

She was clearly lost to her passion, pushing back into his body, meeting him thrust for thrust. "Yes...hard, fast," she panted.

That was all it took and his hips quickened as did his breathing and heart rate. She was pushing back into him, but with each of his thrusts, her body moved closer to the wall. A fine sheen of sweat broke out over his skin. He grabbed her hips and he held her still while her hands braced her upper body.

Her bouncing breasts were a tantalizing shadow on the wall. He glanced away and became mesmerized as his cock disappeared inside her hot little pussy. It was too much. He was going to cum, hard.

The familiar tingle in his spine indicated his orgasm was imminent. No, he wanted it to last longer. He tried to hold back, but her body tightened. She was close and he was unable to stop the inevitable.

He thrust into her like a piston and she cried out his name, her pussy strangling his cock as her climax hit. Dimly, he was aware that her cries had changed, and had become tinged with pain, but he was too overcome with a new and unfamiliar sensation that gripped his shaft. Pleasure and pressure built in the middle of his cock, causing it to swell and lock him inside her body as his orgasm hit and his seed shot into her core. His mind automatically recalled the fact that canine and ursine shifters formed a knot, locking them inside their Fated Mates during intercourse.

Pain seared his forearm, but his hips kept up a slow pace, his body wanting to wring every last ounce of pleasure from them both. He realized that it felt as if his arm had been burned and he glanced down to exam his arm, noticing that Pema was cradling her left arm. The pain intensified and his horrified gaze traveled from her huddled form to his left forearm, sure that he would find it singed to bone. It was hale and whole, but not the same at all.

He tried to pull from her body, but the swelling in his cock locked them together. He lifted his arm and stared down at a brand in the shape of a tribal bear paw, tipped by four crescent moons. The reality of what that meant hit him as his orgasm raged on. The mark and swelling were indicative of a phenomenon that only occurred with a shifter's Fated Mate.

The lust and pleasure was relentless and unabated by the pain of the brand. His release was so intense that he shook all over from the force, and it sent her into another peak. She looked back at him, eyes wide with terror. He roared her name and lifted her close to his body. Her soul rustled in his chest and sent him into another climax. He remained rock hard and locked into her and it seemed the pleasure was going to kill them both. Their bodies may have been reveling in their joining, but mentally they were both freaking out.

As their orgasms waned, the gravity of the situation hit him fully. They were Fated Mates! This witch carried the other half of his soul. The Goddess had made her for him and him for her. This was the female that completed him.

"Holy fucking hell," he muttered ineloquently, as he collapsed to the bed bringing her with him. He was still erect and locked inside her. He rocked gently into her as she sat on his lap. His erection didn't wane in the slightest, despite having had multiple releases. He never wanted to leave her body, he belonged there.

"Oh, Goddess. What happened?" Pema whispered. "I didn't want a mate!"

CHAPTER 8

"What were you thinking?" Cele snapped at her daughter. She was livid. She couldn't think of a time that she'd been angrier. She was, in fact, stunned with disbelief that Claire had been so impetuous. It had been centuries since her daughter had so blatantly disobeyed her. She attempted to calm herself down, to no avail. Her anger was bubbling under the surface, ready to boil over.

Apparently, she hadn't been clear enough when she told her daughter that she needed the triplets alive. Her entire plan depended on them willingly giving their combined power to her. How did Claire think she was going to obtain the power of three if one of them was dead? Without that power, those three trollops could overthrow Cele, and that was intolerable. Cele took deep breaths and sought a calm that continued to eluded her, especially given that her daughter stood entrenched in her justification.

"I was thinking, mother, that I will not allow a Rowan to have my male. You insisted that I end my relationship with him, and like a fool, I listened to you. I will do whatever it takes to correct that mistake!" Claire yelled.

"He is not worthy of you, daughter. Besides, he is not yours. No matter how many centuries you have slept with the beast, the Goddess didn't make him for you. You don't wear his mark," Cele responded crisply, letting all her anger leak into her tone. Her daughter had nearly ruined all her carefully laid plans, and yet she stood there belligerent. It was obvious she had given Claire too much leeway in the past and this behavior wouldn't stand. If she didn't put her daughter in her place, the situation would only escalate.

Cele grabbed her wand off the counter and leveled it at her daughter's chest. "*Tinneasium,*" she spat.

Claire crumpled like an accordion and writhed on the ground for several long minutes, crying and begging for mercy. Cele finally relented and waited for her daughter's contrition. Claire pulled herself up from the floor and met her gaze squarely. She appreciated her daughter's pride and recognized the stubborn tilt to her chin. That wouldn't stop Cele from doing what was necessary to reach her goals. Whether Claire recognized it or not, Cele was doing this for her. One day, she would inherit the power from Cele.

"I will not allow Pema to have him. I have lived in their shadow for too long, and I won't do it anymore! I am your daughter. You should acknowledge my power, too, even if I'm not one of the prophesized three."

That was true and Cele had struggled with Claire and her ability for her entire life. Claire was powerful, but stubborn. It took a lot of persuasion to convince her to hone her craft and when she became obsessed with Ronan, she moved away and didn't portal home often enough. But, from the moment she had learned of the Rowan triplets' birth, Cele had dreamed about negating the prophesy before taking over the Tehrex Realm and unseating Zander, the lofty vampire king and his precious Dark Alliance council.

The realm needed her to reach its full potential. In her opinion, they should stand over humans, not cower in the shadows from them. Zander followed the Goddess' edicts too literally. Cele believed that they were meant to rule the humans and offer protection from evil in exchange for vows of servitude. It disgusted her that such transitory creatures were in charge of the planet.

Cele smiled darkly. The Dark Warriors would be hers to command, and all creatures would bow to her. She would be the most powerful being ever to exist...if her daughter didn't destroy it for her.

"You are my child and need to trust me when I tell you that I will handle the situation. The Rowan triplets aren't to be touched. I will eliminate the shifter before I permit any harm to befall them."

"Don't you dare touch him. I told you he is mine! You taught me that we can't allow an enemy to have anything, that it only gives them strength! And trust me, mother, the Rowans are our enemy," Claire retorted as she plopped down in the high-back chair in Cele's office.

Cele hated that this situation was hurting her daughter, but she wasn't about to give up on obtaining their power. Claire needed to get control of Claire. "Darling daughter, you need to stop. I have explained my plan to harness their magic. I will remind you once more that this plan involves rendering them powerless and completely under my control. After that, Pema is yours to do with as you please. For the time being, none of the Rowan triplets are to be harmed in any way. Do you understand me?"

Claire refused to answer and only glared at her. She saw no respect in the face she loved so much. If Claire didn't respect her, she would certainly fear her. Cele lifted her maple wand again and pointed it at her daughter. "*Tinneasium*," she muttered and felt the vibration of her magic and watched Claire cry out in pain. Cele hardened her heart and watched her daughter hunch over screaming. "I love you daughter, but you will continue to suffer if you refuse to obey me. Do not touch any of the Rowans!" Cele knew her eyes were blazing with her fury and reveled in the way Claire cringed away from her. Her daughter would think twice before disobeying her again.

Claire pleaded with her, tears streaming down her cheeks, "Mother...stop...please." She was sobbing and struggling to sit up. When she saw blood trickle from the corner of Claire's nose, she lowered her wand, and finally ceded.

She circled the desk and cradled her daughter's head, stroking her hair. "Sweetheart, you must listen to me. I know you want Ronan, but you have to leave the situation to me. I don't want to hurt you again, but I will if you force my hand."

Claire's tears continued unchecked and she could feel her trembling beneath her palm. "Yes, mother," she agreed easily, all fight having left her. Cele wondered how long that was going to last. She knew her daughter wouldn't stand by and watch Pema take what she had claimed as her own. Cele needed to find a way to keep Ronan and Pema apart, and force the triplets to give her their powers before that happened.

She gathered her daughter into her arms, cooing in her ear. "Don't worry, my plan will work, darling. I will garner their power and combine it with my own. Pema will be left with nothing."

"No freaking way! That is the best news I've heard since mom's mating," Suvi said in excitement.

Pema sighed, Suvi was such a hopeless romantic. "Yeah, not so much, Suvi. You aren't listening to me. I did not ask for this. The Goddess needs to take this back."

Suvi gasped and placed her hands over her mouth. "Don't say that. Don't ever say that. Fate will make you suffer for such blasphemy. I know you think of this as a curse, but it is a blessing. To be given the chance to find a love that is bigger than the universe, to have that one person who makes you want to unpack your baggage and settle in, is the greatest gift you will ever receive."

"When you think about it, this news isn't really surprising. The signs were all there from the beginning, and I'm shocked we missed them. The chemistry between you two was explosive. Set the drapes on fire explosive. And, Suvi is right, this isn't a curse," Isis added.

"Mom's mating was the worst day of my life. It killed me to see dad so devastated and I vowed to never be a part of anything that would cause someone so much pain. Even if it wasn't intended. I'm having a hard time reconciling how I felt then with how I'm feeling now," Pema responded as she turned and threw out the small stub that remained of the burned incense.

It was hard to disagree completely with her sister when her body was humming with satiation, despite the fact that her head was killing her. The internal battle over this refused to let up and it was giving her a migraine. She was a witch and never got migraines. Fate was surely laughing at her with this one. Rather than steering clear of Ronan, she gave into her desires, and was rewarded with a mate, a mate she didn't want.

She had told herself she would have sex with him the

one time and get him out of her system. Now, the male was as deep in her as any ever would be. She wanted him more with every second that passed, he consumed her every thought. She was in a constant state of arousal and discomfort as a result. His soul rustled in her chest and she glanced down at the brand on her left forearm.

Her mate mark burned painfully and didn't diminish when she traced the outline with a cooling spell. She knew the pain would only worsen until they completed the mating. It was the Goddess' way of ensuring they couldn't deny one another.

She felt the connection to him growing by the minute. In fact, when she concentrated she was able to discern that he was driving through traffic and was as upset as she was over their mating. He hadn't wanted it any more than she did initially, because he had wanted to win Claire back. They hadn't discussed anything before she hastily redressed and found her sisters then left the club so she wasn't certain of his exact stance. But, through their bond, she sensed he was trying to come to terms with being her mate.

It was astonishing to think of how complex the Goddess' plans were. It took many different factors to occur and bring him to Seattle and her doorstep. It proved to her that their meeting was inevitable. She may not have wanted this, but she had it now and needed to find a way to come to terms with this whole situation.

After she ran from Ronan's bed, it had been a long night followed by a long morning. Jace had called with the lab results. His scientists had sampled the remaining drops of liquid left in her glass and confirmed that it had been contaminated with cyanide. The dose had been so concentrated that if she wasn't a supernatural, she would've died before Jace was able to help her.

Claire had poisoned her and if Jace had not been there then she would have died. Pema's anger ignited at the thought and quickly turned to rage. Almost immediately, the ground began to shake as Isis absorbed Pema's emotions. When she spotted a crack appear in the concrete flooring, she employed every calming technique their mother had ever taught her. Steadying her emotions was vital before any more damage was done to their store. Grabbing a stick of incense, she lit the end, praying to the Goddess that it would bring peace and tranquility to the atmosphere.

She checked the time and realized that Ronan would be there soon. That claimed all of her attention and had her blood humming with anticipation. She was happy that the closer he came to her location, the more her anger turned lascivious.

She could try to deny her feelings all she wanted, but she couldn't forget that it felt right to be with him. Her body and both of their souls were crying out for her to go to him and finish the mating. She knew all too well that the torment would only increase until they completed the ceremony.

She rubbed the mating brand on her forearm which burned like acid. The pain increased with her arousal and the question ran through her mind if she could live with the discomfort for the rest of her immortal life. The reality was that if she didn't go forward with this mating, she would never find relief.

She heard the slam of a door and looked out the window to see Ronan crossing in front of his truck. He was sinfully good-looking and even his truck was sexy, she thought ruefully. What was it about a male and his truck?

He walked with confidence and determination. She shivered, even that was a turn-on. She wanted him desperately. There was nothing about him that didn't make her weak. As an independent female, she typically found male power domineering, but the way it seeped from his pores was making her want to give him whatever he demanded. Okay, if she didn't stop mooning like a lovesick puppy, she was going to kick her own ass.

The scariest part about it was that she wanted this shifter more than anything. She chanted a string of denials as she shook her head. They had to talk and if she had her way there would be no conversation. She turned to her sisters and quickly spat, "Get in the office. No, wait, stay here." She was already in way too deep. "I know I sound crazy, and maybe I am."

"We're going to the back. I don't want to see your pink parts, or his. Call us if you need help turning him into a toad, sis," Isis offered then hugged her hard and quick.

"Grab hold of him and don't let go. You deserve happiness, Pema," Suvi whispered into her ear before following Isis to the office.

"Yeah, thanks," she murmured as they stalked to the backroom. She had her back to the door when she heard the wind chime. Her heart began fluttering rapidly like the wings of a hummingbird. That was the sound she had heard the first time he had walked into her life and changed it forever. The sound would forever make her insides melt.

She recalled his woodsy scent, and the way one curl hung over his eye as the sunlight haloed his frame, making her long for completion. She was unprepared for the emotion the memory brought forth. She took a deep breath and steeled her nerves before she turned around.

When she saw him standing in front of her, her breath left her in a whoosh. No male had a right to look so edible.

One thick eyebrow rose over his warm, chocolate-brown eyes. He nervously ran a hand through his thick, curly, brown hair. That stubborn curl dropped back down into his eye and she wanted to brush it away, cup his cheeks then kiss his luscious lips.

Her gaze traveled south in a slow perusal. She hadn't yet allowed herself a good long look at him, and with all she had been through, she figured she deserved it. She was five-foot-nine inches and preferred tall males. Ronan didn't disappoint. He was six feet of muscled glory.

The image of him surging in and out of her as he caged her beneath him flashed in her mind, making her ache. Her mate mark began burning and her abdomen clenched with need. Nothing in her life compared to the way the mating compulsion forced her to recognize what belonged to her. She couldn't deny what her body wanted. That didn't bode well for her willpower or that talk they needed to have. She had questions. Did he still want Claire? How did he feel about their mating? What did they do from here?

Yet, she couldn't make any of that matter at the moment. He had been in the store for all of ten seconds and she wondered why he wasn't already inside her. She prayed to the Goddess for strength. Oh right, the Goddess had placed her in this predicament. There'd be no help from that direction.

She caught him checking her out, too, and suddenly, his nostrils flared and he growled low in his throat. No doubt, he had picked up the scent of her arousal. It was thicker than the sandalwood incense. She'd be embarrassed if she wasn't so busy watching him lick his lips. The sight of his tongue sliding across his full lips had her thinking of what he'd done to her with them the night before. Focusing would be easier if the orgasms he'd given her hadn't literally transported her to the stars. She wanted more of that, what female wouldn't?

Everything about him was animalistic and raw. His glowing stare saw straight to her soul. "Do you still want Claire?" she asked, wishing she didn't sound like a jealous teenager. Tendrils of his arousal, which only enhanced his musky evergreen scent, weakened her resolve and ability to think coherently.

When he didn't answer but only stared at her, she turned away, needing to break the growing tension. He grabbed her arm and spun her back around. When he wrapped his arms around her waist, she went rigid against his chest. Her heart told her that this was where she belonged, but she wasn't sure how he felt.

"Why would you even ask me that?" was his response as he licked his lips hungrily.

"We can't keep doing this." She wasn't going to play this game. Of course, that meant she was leaving him to another female and damning herself to a lifetime of pain. Pain, she realized, she could live with. It was the thought of him being with another female that her soul rebelled against...she'd be damned if she allowed that to happen.

"We will be doing this for eternity...*mate*," he promised and kissed her cheek. Immediately, all thought evaporated as she sought his lips with hers, clawing to get his shirt off. He helped by pulling it over his head and tossed it to the floor. It was like a ravenous beast had taken control over her body.

"Your sweet strawberry scent intensifies with your arousal," he murmured. "I need your taste in my mouth."

She cut him off, "Don't say things like that. You have to leave, we can't do this," she mumbled against his neck where she was licking and kissing and nibbling his flesh.

She told herself to lift her head and step back, but her hands had a mind of their own and began a leisurely perusal up and down his muscled back. His groans filled her ear as he turned his head and licked the shell of her ear then began sucking on her neck.

She almost cried out when he paused to whisper in her ear. "I'm not leaving. I'm as confused as anyone, but there is no denying how I feel about you. On that subject I am perfectly clear."

CHAPTER 9

"You are mine and I am yours. There is no one else, our souls can't deny that truth," Ronan swore. Pema's heart raced from panic and fear as much as it did from arousal. It was like her brain had decided to take a vacation and allow her traitorous body to run the show for the time being. Helpless, she leaned into him as he ran his hand down the curve of her breast, teasing her.

"And, I plan to bury my cock so deep inside you that we don't know where I end and you begin," he rumbled as he ran his hot tongue up her neck.

"Goddess, help me..." Pema never finished her plea. Ronan crushed his mouth over hers, with a kiss that was so hot and forceful that she was entirely at his mercy. He took control, owning her in a way she'd never experienced. It was forceful and demanding with a clash of teeth and tongues, and it thrilled her like nothing else. Her reservations flew out the proverbial window as she gave in, moaning her pleasure, kissing him back. She ran her fingertips along his bare back and sank her fingernails into his flesh.

The sensation of his soul wrapping around hers echoed the way his body encompassed hers, stealing her breath. Through their connection, she felt the bear prowling beneath his skin and it was erotic as hell. She had never had a male come so unhinged over her, and it emboldened her actions.

Without conscious thought, she ground her hips against his erection, bringing his animal even closer to the surface. She wanted to connect with the bear as well, and to do that, she needed to feel him right under his skin. Most shifters buried their animal deep inside while they had sex, for safety reasons. An out of control shifter was dangerous and unpredictable. She didn't want his bear in any corner; she wanted him right under her touch.

She pulled back and saw his eyes clearly this time, they were glowing a brilliant cognac, heavy with lust. Pema arched her back, pressing her body against his hairy chest. He ran his hand down the side of her throat and bare shoulders. His fingers slid into the top of her peasant blouse and slowly pushed it down, revealing her to his gaze.

Her nipples tightened under his scrutiny, a silent plea for attention. She pressed back against him needing the contact, the friction. Each breath she took made her breasts heave, rubbing her nipples tantalizingly against his skin. It caused a flood of wetness to seep from her core. Her craving was intense and undeniable and he had barely touched her.

There was no way she could have been prepared for how intimacy was between mates.

He pulled back and stared at her in shameless hunger. His eyes told her that he wanted her and only her. She loved how her body captivated this male. His fingers danced from her shoulders to her pebbled tips, then pinched and pulled, elongating them further. "Goddess, that feels so good, Ronan. So damn good, it has to be a sin."

"Not a sin, love. Right," he declared and sucked her nipple into his mouth. He was working her flesh like a violin and she loved it. Pema grabbed at his pants and fumbled with the zipper.

He kissed his way to her other breast and pushed her long flowing skirt down over her hips. Her body was on a triple-loop rollercoaster as he skimmed his fingers under the edge of her silk panties. Yes, she silently pleaded. She had been aching for him for two days, and last night hadn't been enough.

She shimmied and the fabric fell to the floor. A bright light blinded her momentarily, reminding her they were in her shop in front of a large picture window. She looked around in a sensual daze, searching for a private place and spotted a fabric chair off to the side. She grabbed his hand and pulled him toward it as she lowered his zipper, freeing his erection, making her mouth water.

Right now, she wanted this male, regardless of anything else. She shoved aside his pants, to fully embrace everything Ronan had to give her. She placed the hand he was teasing her with between her legs. "Feel what you do to me. How hot and wet you make me. It's like that from one glance. I need you...now." He stroked her and the moan that escaped her was deep and throaty.

She reached down and palmed his long, thick cock. "Harder," he demanded. "Squeeze it. Stroke it." His head fell back and he groaned, pumping himself into her hand. Her free hand reached under his shaft and cupped his balls. A firm squeeze had his head snapping forward. He growled as she ran her thumb along the slick slit and increased her rhythm. He impatiently pulled her hands off him and picked her up.

She squealed when he lowered her down onto his cock. The hot wet slide of her flesh over his shaft brought her tantalizingly close to climax. It was nothing for her strong mate to stand there holding her with his cock buried to the hilt inside her core. He nestled his head in the crook of her neck and stood still. Given his labored breathing, she guessed he was trying to regain control of himself.

"Chair...fast," she pointed to the corner. "Goddess help us, but if you don't move soon I may die," she mumbled as her pussy clenched and unclenched around him while he walked to the chair.

"Yes," she hissed out, the motion driving her over the edge as she cried out from her climax.

"That's it, come hard for me, baby," he replied, licking her nipple as he sank down into the chair, keeping his cock seated inside her.

∼

Ronan was inside his mate and she had just come on his aching cock. The hot slide in and out of her sweet pussy brought him unimaginable pleasure. He wanted to remain buried inside this perfect female for days. He had been afraid and confused after they had been together. He'd had a carefully laid out plan to win Claire back, but all that changed after he discovered she had poisoned Pema. And, then he learned Pema was his Fated Mate.

He refused to hold onto the past and was determined to be with Pema. He'd been given the gift of his Fated Mate and didn't plan on squandering it. He hated that his previous relationship with Claire was placing walls between them. He planned on tearing them down brick by brick because every moment he spent with Pema made him fall for her even more. He wanted to claim his mate and all that entailed.

He wrapped his arms around Pema as his protective instinct took hold. No one would harm her ever again. He would die before he let that happen. In the meantime, his hands slid down and gripped her ass, moving her up and down. His pace was slow, but when she gasped and dug her nails into the flesh of his back, he increased his pace, pounding into her. Her channel rippled around him, and that fast, she was close again.

She may deny what was happening between them, but her response gave him hope for the future. She was as affected by him as he was by her. She threw her head back and took control, riding him hard. He leaned down and sucked her nipple as he reached between their bodies and found her clit. He gave it a pinch and she came with a rush, screaming his name. *His name.* He wanted to pound his chest in triumph.

He closed his eyes. Nothing existed in that moment but them. As the hot wash of Pema's climax drowned his cock, Ronan knew the true feeling of love and family. His teeth elongated into his bear's fangs, and for the first time, he realized the true pain of needing to claim his mate.

He gritted his teeth against the desire. She would never forgive him if he proceeded with the mating and took her blood. His arm was on fire, but none of it diminished his pleasure and was easily pushed aside. They didn't belong in that moment. They would complete the mating soon, he told himself.

He watched his cock disappear deeper into the slick haven between her legs. He caressed her ass cheeks and slid his finger into the crevasse. He reached her core and coated his finger in her moisture. He wasn't going to begin the blood exchange like his body demanded, but did he dare give into his animal and claim her dark passage? She went wild, bucking when his finger teased her backside and slowly entered the tight opening. He worked her clit with one hand and finger-fucked her ass with the other while he sucked her breast and thrust into her.

His spine tingled and his seed surged into his shaft. The middle of his cock filled with blood and the mating knot became engorged, locking him to his mate. The mating knot enhanced his pleasure to an unbelievable level. "Someday, Pema, I will have all of you," he vowed, his breath coming in pants now. He pistoned in and out of her as much as the knot allowed.

"Yes," she cried out as she peaked again. Her body demanded he give up his seed and he was powerless to deny it. He lifted his head, desperate to see her sea-green pools filled with rapture as he erupted. He held her close while he drove into her with shallow thrusts, frantic now to reach that peak with her. Before she came down from her third peak, he rolled his hips and pulled her tighter to his body.

Unable to hold back any longer, he exploded, his seed spilling into the mouth of her womb. He ground against her harder and she came once again. He was surprised when his thoughts shifted to wondering if they would get a child out of this union. He knew the swelling meant that he was now fertile and for the first time in his long life, he longed for a family with this precious female who had been made solely for him.

He met Pema's glowing sea-green eyes. She was so beautiful, his heart ached to have her completely. "One day soon I will claim you for always," he guaranteed.

CHAPTER 10

Pema watched Ronan pull away from the curb in front of Black Moon, wondering when she was going to see him again. She was powerless against the mating compulsion and relished that every encounter only brought them closer together. She was falling for Ronan and didn't care that she was vulnerable to heartache and loss. She hadn't wanted to be a part of something that had crushed her father's heart, leaving him a broken male, but the pull was undeniable.

None of her questions mattered because she knew for certain that he wanted only her. His declarations went a long way to settling her uncertainty. The fact of the matter was that they had both been permanently transformed and there was no going back.

The glare from a car window had her shielding her eyes. As she turned to call her sisters from the office, she caught a glimpse of a grey Mercedes driving away. Doing a double take, she thought she saw a female with mousy-brown hair that looked exactly like Claire's. If that witch thought to harm her again, she had another thing coming. Don't jump to conclusions, her inner voice chided. The poisoning must be making her paranoid, there was no way it had been Claire.

She heard the click of the back door followed by her sisters' footsteps. "Damn, I can't believe you rode him like a bronco in the front of our store. You're lucky someone didn't walk in, but I'm proud of you," Suvi crowed. "We need to get you a rope and boots, with spurs. Giddy-up girl," Suvi whooped, spinning her finger in a circle above her head as she exited the office, followed by Isis.

"He is magnificent," Pema sighed looking out the window. "The Goddess has blessed me with a talented mate and I can't help myself when he is near." Her world was spinning on its axis and she was excited for what would come next.

"Magnificent he may be, sister, but you showed your bare ass to half of Seattle," Isis remarked as she leaned against a display case. "And, we need to send this chair out to have it cleaned. I can't sit on it knowing what you guys did. How about the next time you do the shifter, you put a towel down first," Isis teased.

She needed to keep her hands off the male, not start fantasizing about the next time. Her mate mark began to itch and burn as her desire rose. "We don't need to worry about that. We never actually made it into the chair," she said rubbing at the pain in her arm.

"I am the worst sister on the planet" she gestured wildly with her hands, "I didn't once consider how my actions will impact you both and I think I saw Claire drive by the shop after he left. What if she hurts one of you because of me?" Pema asked, outraged by her selfishness.

Her first concern had always been for her sisters. Yet, she had put them in danger of coming into Claire's crosshairs and hadn't once given a thought as to how to protect them. She'd been too busy having mind-numbing sex with her mate.

"You are not responsible for what Claire does. We can protect ourselves," Suvi declared, fixing a display of potions. "I love seeing you so happy. You positively glow, Pema. I can't wait to find my mate. It all sounds so delicious. And I hope he's a vampire like Bhric. I love fangs…" As her sister trailed off, smoke rose from Suvi's silver ring and became her familiar, a black bat that she named Bhric, of all things. It launched itself and landed on Suvi's shoulder, nuzzling her ear. "Hello, my sweet," she petted the bat absently, lost in a daydream.

Isis rolled her eyes at them both. "You worry too much, sis, Suvi is right. We can take care of Claire, if she tries anything. In fact, I'm rather hoping she will try something."

Isis tilted her head to the side and considered Pema. "Did you realize that your powers were flaring while you rode your honey bear? Suvi and I contained it, but it could have ended up causing damage."

Pema contemplated what she was saying. She hadn't been aware that her power had surged. Losing control of her magic was dangerous. Not only that, power flares could be harnessed in the right vessel. The last thing she wanted was to add power to anyone's arsenal.

"I think if you don't complete the mating, you had better avoid sex with him unless we are close. Not that I mind, he does have a nice ass," Suvi said, waggling her eyebrows comically.

Beyond Pema's control, her jealousy spiked, regardless of the fact that her sister was teasing. Still, she couldn't help but responding, "If you look at my male again, I'll gouge your eyes out. He's mine." Ronan's soul flexed in her chest, sending warmth coursing through her body, like a shot of tequila, only magnified.

"Clearly your hormones have hijacked your brain. This is day two of Pema's mental vacation and you need to get it together," Isis added.

"Problem is I don't have control. This mating has wreaked havoc with me," she grabbed Isis up into a quick hug. "It's not easy, but I promise you, I am trying."

Pema's stomach chose that moment to growl in the quiet of the store. "I'm famished. You guys want Vietnamese?"

"I'd be famished too if I'd been working my mate as hard as you have," Suvi sang out and started giggling. Pema couldn't help but smile at her sister, she wasn't wrong.

"I'll take the lemongrass beef with egg and crushed rice," Suvi requested.

Suvi's infectious laughter had Isis giggling behind her hand. "That sounds fantastic. I'll take the grilled pork and vermicelli with some egg rolls, please. You sure you can manage after that rough ride? Do you need help to your car?" Isis teased.

"Smart ass," Pema replied as she picked up her purse and walked toward the door. She retrieved her car keys and paused on her way to the door, ducking the pen Isis had thrown. She smiled over her shoulder at her sister.

When she turned back around she noticed that it was pouring outside. She used her remote to unlock the doors and a loud explosion sounded, followed by blinding fire. The force of the blast threw her against a glass display case and glass shattered, flying towards her.

She felt like a rag doll being tossed around. She could feel cuts all over her body, but had no idea how severe they were. Her head hit the concrete floor, causing stars to wink in her vision and sharp pain to sear her brain.

The world went dark and when Pema came to, smoke filled the room and she was disoriented. She had no idea how long she had been out of it, but felt a burning sensation in her limbs. Her sisters' screams filled her ears and she tried to move toward them, but her body refused to obey.

She lay panting for long moments while the noise settled and her sisters went quiet. Frantic, she shouted their names, but they didn't respond to her. Fear twisted her gut at the thought of them being injured. Only one person could have done this. She had no doubt that it was Claire. It was Pema's fault that her sisters were hurt. They had to be alive or she would never forgive herself.

Warm liquid dripped off her arms from a million tiny cuts that littered her exposed skin. She turned to look at her legs and groaned. As she tried to lift her head, it throbbed and felt like a lead balloon. She sat still, gathering her strength and trying to clear the dizziness.

When the pressure in her head eased a bit, she lifted her eyes and realized her left arm had gone through the glass case and was stuck in the broken doors of the display cabinet. She finally managed to glance down and then wished she hadn't. Bones were sticking out of her right arm and left thigh. Oddly, it didn't hurt nearly as bad as she thought it should. She was sure that shock kept most of the pain at bay.

She tried to cast a pain-relieving spell so she could get to her sisters, but nausea assailed her. Silence descended over the room, or maybe she had blacked out again, she couldn't be sure. Smoke, thick and cloying, poured in through the missing front windows. Her beautiful Ferrari was in flames at the curb.

Anger, hot and sharp, had her cursing. She began coughing and grimaced at the pain in her rib cage. She added a broken rib to her list of injuries and wondered again if her sister were okay. As much as her injuries allowed, she searched the rubble for sight of them.

Unable to see anything, it took every ounce of strength to pull her left arm free. Her attempt to stand up brought sharp pain and made her stumble. Her leg gave out and she fell back down. Thankfully, Isis crawled to her side and Suvi was right behind her.

"Thank the Goddess. Are you guys okay?" Pema asked as she laid her head back and saw Bhric, Suvi's bat, flying erratically overhead.

"Pema...holy shit, your arm! Oh Goddess, your leg, don't move! I'm going to put pressure on them and it's going to hurt. Suvi, call Jace and see if he can portal here," Isis ordered. Pema knew it was bad if they wanted Jace to portal to her. The pain now wracking her body only confirmed her suspicions. She cried out when Isis pressed on her injuries.

Isis' eyes hardened like a storm-laden sky as she snarled, "I'm going to find that bitch and kill her. She isn't getting away with it this time. She has fucked with the wrong witches!" Before Pema could agree with her sister's rant, Isis' grip tightened and her world went black.

∽

RONAN DROVE BACK to his apartment in the pouring rain, replaying the sex with Pema. He was awed by the experience and anxious for more. His mate was a hellcat and fired his blood like no other. The change his thinking had undergone in a matter of hours was mind-boggling. He had gone from not being sure what he wanted, to wanting nothing but Pema.

His cell phone rang, interrupting his thoughts. Caller ID

told him it was the hotline at Zeum. This was the first number he had been given when he arrived in Seattle right after Killian had explained the state of affairs with the demons and skirm. Immediately, he began to worry. Why would the Dark Warriors be calling him? Was it Pema?

"This is Ronan Blackwell." His bear stirred as his anxiety rose.

A deep, male voice answered his greeting. "Ronan, this is Rhys at Zeum. I need to talk to you about something. Is this a good time?"

"Sure. How can I help you?" Silence met his reply. He waited several agonizing seconds and wanted to reach through the phone and punch the shit out of the male and make him talk.

Just when he was about to lose it with the Dark Warrior, he said the words that had Ronan's stomach dropping to his feet. "There's been an explosion at Black Moon."

He had left his mate there not fifteen minutes ago. Goddess, how did this happen? He should never have left. His instinct had been roaring at him to stay by her side to protect her and he had ignored it. He would never forgive himself if something had happened to her. His bear roared in outrage.

"Was anyone hurt? Is Pema okay? Her sisters?" He wasn't accustomed to worrying, yet was besieged by it at the moment.

"The only people in the store at the time were the triplets. Isis and Suvi are fine, minor cuts and scratches. Pema, however, was seriously injured. She was taken by ambulance to Harborview where Jace is treating her," Rhys replied somberly.

Ronan sucked in a breath, already turning the truck around to head across town. "Will she be alright?" He forced the question through a throat closed off by his churning emotions. The full impact that his mate was injured hit him and he nearly lost control of his vehicle. An overwhelming need to get to her side had him snarling. He needed to see her and hold her in his arms.

"She is going to be fine. I just got off the phone with Jace, who said she suffered several broken bones, a concussion and numerous internal injuries. She will be discharged soon and Zander has invited her and her sisters to stay at Zeum until we can find the ones responsible," Rhys paused and took a breath. "I'm calling you because I noticed you carried her off to a room last night and today she has a mate mark... I assume it's yours."

"Yes, she's mine. I'm on my way. And I appreciate you guys offering up Zeum to her. I need her safe while I take care of something," Ronan said, suspicion blooming about who was responsible for this.

He had spoken to Claire after the poisoning and the venom in her denial about trying to kill Pema belied her words. He felt her hatred through the phone and knew that it was deeper than she was letting on. He had recalled over the past couple decades that she would complain about the triplets after she would return from visiting her mother, but he had never given it much thought. Now, he could see that this animosity was greater than simple jealousy.

"I can imagine what you are thinking since I feel your anger and bloodlust through the phone. Trust me. Neither choice is a smart one right now. Pema mentioned Claire and we have Isis under wraps for the same reasons. Claire's mother is very powerful and has powerful allies. You don't want to stir that hornet's nest."

"Oh, that's where you are wrong, warrior. I want to beat the shit out of it at the moment. No one harms my mate and gets away with it. She will pay," he barked into the phone. He had to see for himself that his mate was alright and then take care of matters.

"Look, I know it's hard right now, but you need to calm down and find an outlet other than revenge at the moment. If you go after her and they manage to take you out, then you are leaving your mate completely vulnerable. I know you don't want that, right?"

He knew the Dark Warrior was right, but his bloodlust wouldn't be denied. His safety didn't matter, only his mate's. Besides, he always cleaned up his messes, and if not for him, Pema wouldn't have been injured and nearly killed twice. This was far from over.

CHAPTER 11

Ronan drove recklessly through downtown Seattle, having just ended his call with Rhys. Pema had been injured again and he needed to get to her. He concentrated on his connection to his mate and headed in the direction he felt she was, but he had no idea exactly where the infamous Dark Warrior compound was. No matter how hard he tried, he wasn't able to pin point her exact location. His bear was clawing at his skin to break free, confident it could find her anywhere in this city.

He glanced at the cell phone in the seat next to him. Rhys had been spot-on that Ronan needed to calm down before doing anything rash, which was difficult to do when he was being assaulted by so many foreign emotions. Things with Pema had been hard and fast and intense, so it was no surprise that he had fallen for her. He realized as he agonized over what to do that he loved her and didn't care that he had gone from zero to sixty and left his past behind.

He needed to make sure Pema was protected. They had a life to begin together, and he'd be damned if he was going to let anything interfere with that. He only wished that his family was there to meet his Fated Mate. Sadness swamped him when he thought of them. They would have loved her fire and wit.

His bear once again clawed at the surface, wanting out. Every cell in his body screamed with the desire for vengeance. The knowledge that he failed his mate cut him to the bone. Never again, he vowed. He'd make sure she had everything she could ever want. Her smiles and happiness were all that mattered.

An image of her astride him with a sated smile gracing her lips flashed into his mind, casting the shadows away. He wasn't able to stop the memory as it traveled through their entire interlude. They were combustible together, and always would be. She fired his blood like nothing else.

He wanted nothing more than to forget his out of control bear and his need for vengeance to find his mate and make love to her. Physical pain and discomfort from their unfinished mating battered him, pushing him to seek Pema out and finish their mating. Unless they completed the mating with a blood exchange, their pain would become unbearable.

As the streets passed by in a blur, his bear clamored even more to be let loose and take action. Controlling his animal at the moment was one of the most difficult challenges he'd ever faced. He rubbed his mate mark and thought about fate and the Goddess. He sent a prayer of thanks to the Goddess for making Pema for him.

With that in mind, he had work to do. Finally able to think more clearly, he decided that first he would shift and hunt, releasing his aggression. A hunt would have to substitute for vengeance until a plan could be devised that didn't put Pema at risk again. He and his bear were in agreement that his mate being in danger was unacceptable.

Killian had told him that Claire and her mother were dangerous, and he wasn't tackling that issue without seeking advice and a plan. On that note, he picked up his cell phone from the seat and called his Omega. He wasn't leaving his mate without all the protection at his disposal.

"Hayden here." The deep burly voice of his Omega was a welcomed relief.

"Hayden, its Ronan Blackwell. I'm not sure if you've heard about what happened, but I have a situation that I need help with." Ronan gripped the steering wheel tightly, nearly bending the steel.

"'Bout time you realized I'm here to help. No doubt, you're calling about your mate…a witch named Pema Rowan. If my information is correct, I believe there was an explosion and she and her sisters are currently staying at Zeum," his leader said, evenly.

Ronan was shocked, having no idea that Hayden was that well connected. Ronan had just learned of the events himself, but after all, Hayden was the Omega and sat on a council with several other leaders in the realm. Of course he would be informed about an incident of such importance.

"Your information isn't wrong, about any of it. I have to tell you that my ex, Claire, is responsible, and my bear is clawing at me to shred her for what she has done then take her head to Pema. I have to eliminate the threat to Pema, but can't just yet, and my bear is close to breaking free…" Ronan trailed off, wiping the sweat from his brow. The continuous battle to keep his animal caged was rubbing him raw.

"Be still," Hayden ordered, shifter-magic layering his voice. As the Omega, Hayden had the ability to shift into any animal, and the power behind that enabled him to gain control of any of his shifters. Immediately, Ronan's bear backed off at hearing the command in his leader's voice. He had never had to call on Hayden, and the experience of having his bear cowed by this strong leader was disturbing. It wasn't something he ever wanted to need again, because for a split second, it was almost as if his bear was gone.

However, Ronan was grateful the powerful male was behind him in this matter, and that he could count on him. Hayden would come in handy when it came time to exact his revenge.

"I have been in contact with Zander and several other members of the council about the poisoning and the bombing," Hayden continued. "Luckily, Pema was able to provide the make, model and partial license plate of a car seen driving away from the scene right before the explosion. Otherwise, there would be no evidence to support your claim that Claire is responsible. Don't even think of going after Claire. As Pema's mate, you may have the right to seek revenge without risk of punishment for murder, but we need to develop a plan first. You will not go into this half-cocked. The High Priestess is not an enemy the shifters want. Do you understand?"

There was no mistaking the command in those statements. It chafed, but Ronan understood there was a larger picture to consider. He wasn't good at sitting back and talking about doing something. He needed to take action and endless hours of sitting in meetings just to develop a plan would drive him insane. He believed in kicking ass and taking names, he could ask questions later.

For him, ensuring Pema's safety was paramount, and the rest could go to hell. Still, he had no choice but to follow the order, "Yes, sire. I understand."

"So, what can I do for you in the meantime?" Hayden asked.

A fierce pain stabbed through his arm to his heart and

soul. The need to be with his mate and claim her fully stole his breath momentarily. "I need you personally to watch out for Pema and add security to what Zander is already providing. I'm going to let my bear out for a hunt, but I can't do that unless I know she is guarded while I'm in the woods. Also, I'd appreciate it if you can make sure her shop is secured."

Hayden chuckled. "I will see to it right away. Zander and I are meeting with the council in fifteen. We all need to be on alert, and assume Cele is a threat, as well. Go get your head on straight then get your ass to Zeum. I'll text you the address."

"Thank you, sire," Ronan replied before he clicked off.

When he looked around, he realized he was already across the bridge and nearing his newfound hunting grounds. A few minutes later, he pulled off Woodinville-Duvall road and parked on a dirt road. He stretched and sent his senses outward, searching for any sign of humans. When he was assured he was alone with the creatures of the forest, he shed his clothes, leaving them on the seat of his truck.

The magic of transformation enveloped him and in seconds his animal took over, leaving him on all fours. He let out the roar he had been holding in and charged off into the trees. Soaring evergreens crowded him and lush foliage met his paws. He inhaled the crisp autumn air and took in the scent of the forest, pine and earth. Unfortunately, while it invigorated him, it did little to soothe his boiling rage.

He ran as fast and as far as he could, clawing tree after tree, felling them. Panting, he approached a stream for a drink of water. As he lapped up the liquid, foreign magic rippled over his fur, causing it to stand on end. This wasn't friendly magic, it had a menacing taint to it. Every instinct told him that danger was near. This would do nicely for the hunt both male and bear needed.

On silent paws, he padded through the underbrush and followed his nose. Soon, the stench became unbearable. It was a putrid combination of rotten eggs, brimstone and fresh blood. Ronan had to bite back his growls. Aside from his knife-sized claws, stealth and surprise were his best weapons.

Peeking around a large tree trunk, he saw two enormous, hideous, black dog-like creatures that were bigger than a Clydesdale. Being twice the size of a normal grizzly, he wasn't intimidated. He had no idea what they were; yet somehow, his bear identified them as hellhounds. The male inside had no frame of reference for what the bear knew instinctively, but he had learned long ago to trust his bear's intuition.

The scent of fresh blood came from the deer they were feeding on. He crouched and took their measure. They were vicious, fighting each other for the kill. He could use their infighting to his advantage. As he tensed to attack, Pema's soul stretched and he swore it purred in his chest. He smiled at the thought that his witch was a warrior and excited about the coming battle. She was a fierce and passionate female all the way around, and he loved it.

Blood pumping and adrenaline flooding his brain, Ronan charged into the small space. Before the creatures were aware of anything, he had barreled into one of them and clamped his teeth down into its slick flesh. Thrashing his head from side to side, he separated its head from its body. A disgusting, foul taste lingered on his tongue and he realized that he had the hellhound's head in his mouth and the blood was seeping down his throat. He had never tasted anything so vile. His gut churned and he dropped the head, turning to face the other hound that was prowling toward him.

He bared his canines and let loose his growls. They circled each other, stepping over debris. He swiped out one dinner-plate-sized paw and connected with a flank. The hound howled and broke formation to charge him. He tried to side step the hit, but the huge beast was too fast. Searing pain in his left shoulder had Ronan staggering. It felt like acid had been injected into his flesh. Pushing the pain aside, he tried to clear his head.

Claws scrabbling in the pine needles and dried leaves of the forest floor caught Ronan's attention. He looked to the left and saw the hellhound reverse course and come at him again. He turned as fast as he could, but his injury slowed him down. He couldn't allow the thing to land another hit, so he mustered all the energy he could for an attack. He reached out with his right paw and missed. The demon-dog danced out of the way and the move tore open its flank wound, which began bleeding black again.

Ronan needed to use his surroundings to his advantage. He scanned the area, then ran past the hound's left side and pushed off on his hind legs to hit a tree about five feet off the ground. He gritted his teeth against the pain when his front paws were jarred by the action. Ignoring that, he used his rear legs to push back off the tree. He twisted in mid-air and landed on the stunned creature. He dug his claws into its sides with all his remaining strength. Unlike his opponent, Ronan's wound was not healing and black dots were marring his vision. Something was preventing his rapid healing process from beginning.

As Ronan geared up to finish the demon-dog, it twisted in his hold, tearing through its own shark-like skin. Burning pain scalded Ronan's sides as razor sharp teeth pierced his skin. The pain was so intense he almost blacked out. Each drop of hellhound saliva into his flesh felt as if a hot brand was being shoved into his muscle. He writhed and slashed and gnashed at the creature underneath him.

Pema's soul sent warmth flooding through him, blessedly numbing his pain. It gave him the strength to remove his claws and pin the hound's shoulders to the dirt, then he leaned down and sliced through an artery with his incisors. Not wanting anymore of the foul blood in his stomach, he moved his head aside as it gushed from the hellhound's torn neck. He was tired and hurt all over. He had to end this, now. One last swipe of his claws removed the creature's head, ending the battle.

Ronan collapsed to the side and lay panting for several long minutes. He tried to stand up and wasn't able to. What the hell was going on? Normally, he'd be able to shrug this off and recover quickly, but there was no brushing this off. His shoulder and side were still bleeding and on fire. Blackness crept in, telling him he was going to lose consciousness. He needed to get some help or he wasn't going to make it.

After several attempts, he was on all fours and limping back to his truck. As he reached the door, he closed his eyes and pictured Pema laughing with her sisters. She hadn't laughed for him yet, and he wanted that as much as he wanted to claim her. He loved her, and wanted to tell her. He wanted a life and cubs with her. Gathering his strength, he managed to shift and grab his cell phone. He dialed Hayden then oblivion closed in.

~

RONAN ABRUPTLY AWOKE, enveloped by cold water. He inhaled several lungful's of the liquid before he sat up and coughed, expelling the water. His vision was blurry, but he heard familiar voices. Hayden was there with Jace and a couple of Hayden's lieutenants. Where was he and why didn't he remember anything? He blinked, clearing his eyes and focused on Jace, who was hovering over him. He tried to stand up, but he was weak as a cub and fell back onto his ass. Memories of the fight with the hellhounds came flooding back as the pain in his body registered.

"Hey, Ronan, don't move. I need to get these wounds sealed and stop the bleeding. I will have to stitch some of them, but I need to get you cleaned so I can see what is what. You are covered in blood and...demon slime?" Jace's voice lifted at the end in clear question, as he laid his warm hands on Ronan's side.

"Pema," Ronan croaked out. "How is she? Is she safe?" He had to know that she was alive and safe, nothing else mattered.

"Relax, she is doing well. Better than you, I'd wager. I was able to heal all her injuries and she is with her sisters at Zeum," Jace replied continuing his assessment.

"She warned us that something was wrong with you before your call came in. I just spoke with her and let her know we found you," Hayden added from the side of the stream. Only then did he realize that he was in the stream and that Jace was knee deep in the cold water with him.

"We need to move you to the truck. Your shoulder and side will have to be stitched. Unfortunately, my healing power does nothing against the venom in the wounds. What did you encounter out here?" Jace asked the question directly this time.

The nod sent pain winging through his skull and he almost lost his dinner. Jace reached down and helped him stand up. "Thanks. I had just let my bear out for a run when a foreign magic caught me off guard. It was the oddest thing, appearing between one breath and the next. Anyway, I followed the malignant magic and the stench and came across two hellhounds. I didn't know what they were, but my bear somehow did. Long story short, we battled, I won. Their remains are about ten minutes north-west of here."

"Any landmarks we can use to find them?" Hayden asked.

"That direction," Ronan pointed over his shoulder and hissed at the agony the movement caused. "Follow the stench, you can't miss it."

"We'll take care of it and meet you back at your truck," Hayden said.

Ronan and Jace were walking out of the stream, closing the distance between them. "Sure thing, but, if you're here, who is with Pema?" Dizziness almost had him passing out and he shook his head to clear it.

"Pema is fine. The Vampire King and several Dark Warriors are with her. And, there is a contingent of shifters surrounding Zeum. You will be with her soon enough," Hayden related before he headed off through the trees.

Back at the truck, he sat on the tailgate and watched Jace retrieve his medical kit. As the healer prepped everything, Ronan closed his eyes and focused on the fact that he was going to be with Pema soon.

CHAPTER 12

Pema tossed a broken jar into the trash and took in the destruction that surrounded her. She wiped her dusty hands on her blue jeans, tears filling her eyes. The store she and her sisters had worked so hard for was in ruins, and it was all because of her and her mate.

It was her job to take care of her sisters, and here she was the reason they nearly lost their lives. It made her feel even worse that they didn't blame her, but were planning to avenge her. She glanced over and saw Isis was near the front, sweeping the safety glass into a pile while Suvi held a shovel like a dust pan.

"Are you kidding me Suvi?" Pema asked incredulous, noticing for the first time what her sister was wearing.

"What?" Suvi paused and looked up.

Isis stopped, as well, and leaned on the broom with a smirk on her face. "The shoes, Suvi. Only you would wear platform sandals to clean up after a bomb blast," Isis said with a chuckle.

Suvi picked up her foot and turned it this way and that.

"These are my everyday-schlepping-around-shoes. Plus, my toes are drying. I just had a pedicure."

"No, those would be my going-out-on-the-town-shoes. *These* are everyday shoes," Pema said as she pointed to her black and white Converse.

They all burst out laughing before resuming their tasks. Pema glanced around and walked over to the destroyed RockCandy jewelry display. She wanted to burst into tears when she saw that they had lost everything. She knew her sisters were watching her and talking about the same, but she ignored them or she would lose it.

Claire's name caught her attention and she listened to them plotting which instantly dried her tears and spiked her anger. Claire had tried to kill her again! This time, she had enough evidence to provide the elders with proof of her culpability. Thank the Goddess she caught sight of the car and license plate number. The partial, along with the make and model, allowed Killian to work his magic on the computer and connect the car to Claire. That was enough in the Tehrex Realm to convict her of attempted murder. Things in their world didn't work like they did in the human world.

She refused to allow Claire to ruin her life, which was why she and her sisters had refused to stay at Zeum any longer. They needed to get back to business and to do that they needed to clean up the ruins of Black Moon. Of course, a contingent of shifters and Dark Warriors had followed them. The Vampire King had refused to take any chances with their safety. She didn't object, wanting all the help she could get with the repairs.

Ronan had found her knee-deep in rubble two hours ago. Automatically, her eyes traveled back to her sexy shifter. Ronan's lithe body and bulging muscles rippled in his tight red t-shirt and low-slung black jeans as he and Hayden hung plywood over the empty window frames. The sight made her heart race and her abdomen clench with need as her core ached to have him fill her.

She noted that his injuries weren't healing as they should have been and cringed when she recalled him telling her about his fight with two hellhounds. Realm leaders were worried that there were portals between realms appearing and disappearing. Apparently, the Vampire Prince, Kyran, had been running from a burning house and slipped through a portal, vanishing into thin air with a human female over his shoulder. No one had heard from him since, or knew where he was.

This latest appearance of hellhounds had the leaders deep in discussion. There had been a huge battle between Dark Warriors and numerous demons and hellhounds, and it wasn't a good sign that there were still demons coming through the veil to earth.

Pema refocused on the activity around her. Ronan had put significant effort into making sure their shop was restored. She fell more in love with him. No one besides her sisters, had ever worried so much about her, and it was nice. She was beginning to understand some of what her mother must have felt. She didn't want to sympathize with her mom and was still angry that her father was hurt, but it was there, nonetheless.

After the wood was in place, Ronan turned, sensing her eyes on him, and crossed to her side. Like always when they were together, the rest of the world dropped away. They stood there silently staring at each other, his gaze revealing all the desire and love he felt for her. He reached out and wrapped her in his arms and cupped her cheeks. It was one of the most intimate moments of her life, and she realized that she loved him.

She inhaled his wonderfully masculine, pine scent. It went straight to her head, making her body molten and her arousal instantly painful. She needed him more than she needed to breathe, and for the first time she *wanted* to complete their mating. Ronan was a passionate male and it was obvious to her how much he loved her. The biggest factor in his favor was that it wasn't merely the biology of the mating compulsion driving him, he truly saw *her*. She feared opening herself to loss, but realized true loss would be not having him at all.

But first, she had to take care of Claire. She wasn't going to live with that danger hanging over them.

Ronan rubbed his thumb across her jaw and leaned down, kissing her lightly on the lips. "I can see your wheels churning. While your determination is sexy as hell, put whatever you are planning out of your head."

Irritation blazed through her. He may be her mate, but he still had a few things to learn about her. She wasn't putting anything aside or letting anything go. "That's not going to happen, but you don't need to worry. Everything will be fine. My sisters and I will handle it."

"I don't like the sound of that, love. I don't want you doing anything crazy," he gazed intently into her eyes, "like challenging Claire. I'm told that she and her mother are very powerful witches. Don't do anything on your own. We have people to help us deal with them. I couldn't stand it if you were hurt."

He brought his lips back to hers and this time he kissed her soundly. She gave herself over to the wet slide of their tongues, wanting more when he stopped and pulled away.

His eyes were bright cognac with his desire for her. "I love you, Pema. You are my life."

She stood there stunned beyond belief. Through their connection, she felt the sincerity of his words and tears sprang to her eyes. "I love you too, Ronan," she declared, shocked by the truth of her words, "but I need to finish this before we can be together."

"Those three little words have never meant more to me than coming from you. What we have," he said, gesturing between them, "is the most precious gift the Goddess bestows, and you can't jeopardize that by doing what you are thinking. You are talented, yes, but you aren't invincible. Claire's mother has centuries of untold experience. You risk yourself, and understand that if something happens to you, I can't be responsible for what I would do. I would destroy the world if you weren't in it," he replied, wrapping her in a hug and holding her tight, as if he was afraid she would bolt on him.

She gently cupped his stubbled cheek and met his warm chocolate gaze squarely. "You underestimate me. Besides, I have something they don't. The power of three, baby," she boasted, nodding to her sisters.

"Hell yeah, she does," answered Suvi, moving her neck around to punctuate her words.

"Together, we are the most powerful witches alive, Ronan. United, no one can beat us. And I, for one, have some payback to mete out. That bitch almost killed my sister twice and she wrecked our shop," Isis vented through gritted teeth.

Ronan glared at her sisters and picked her up. She gladly wrapped her legs around his hips, resting her hands on his broad shoulders.

"Mark my words, I will not risk my mate's life, end of

discussion," Ronan told her and her sisters. She felt him tremble with his emotions, and knew she couldn't push him on this.

"Mark my words, *mate*, everything is up for discussion." She kissed him feverishly and pulled back when the others began hooting and hollering. "But, I promise not to do anything that will put me in danger." With her sisters on her side, she had no worries about facing Claire.

~

SEVERAL HOURS LATER, Pema stood back and perused the containment circle she and her sisters had set into the earth of the Japanese Garden. It had been a gamble when she had stolen Ronan's cell phone and used it to send Claire a message asking her to meet at this location.

She felt guilty for deceiving Ronan and placing him under a sleep spell, but she didn't feel like she had any other choice. He wouldn't allow her to do what needed to be done, and she didn't want him caught in the middle. She and her sisters were going to try and get a confession, but Pema knew it wasn't going to be that easy.

This battle was going to be about magic, not brute force. Ronan had no way to protect against it and Pema would be too distracted, worrying about what might happen to him. She needed all her focus on the coming battle. Taking care of Claire was the only way for them to proceed with their mating.

The circle was hidden, and since Claire wasn't a strong witch, hopefully she wouldn't detect anything before she was trapped in the middle of it. Pema tucked her wand in the back waistband of her jeans and zipped up her jacket, shielding herself against the cold of a fall night in Seattle.

She was nervous about doing this spell without her usual accoutrements. There would be no candles, herbs, altars or athames. They had to rely solely on their power, and the fact that it was close to a full moon. A full moon would have given them more power, but Pema didn't want to wait even one more day.

"Tell me again why we can't just kill her? Why the truth spell?" Isis glanced around the park expectantly. She had disagreed with this whole set-up, saying they should eliminate her altogether.

"If we kill her then that makes us no better than her. I refuse to be anything like her. Getting her to admit what she did will seal her fate. I want the elders to have everything they need. Cele is manipulative, and will find a way out of this for her daughter. We are going to make sure she can't. Are you ready to record this, Suvi?" The ferocity of her feelings surprised even her. Her blood hummed with anticipation, she was ready to get this over with. Checking the time on her cell phone, she noted Claire should be there in five minutes.

"I was born ready," Suvi said with a wink, holding up her phone. Pema loved her sisters as much as she loved Ronan. From the moment they were born, they had shared a connection that rivaled that of the mating bond. There wasn't anything they wouldn't do for one another, even murder, if Isis had her way.

"Thanks sis, now you two need to go get behind those trees and shield your presence," she replied, pointing to some maples a few yards away. "She won't approach if she sees us together and we need her in the circle. Come out after she activates it." Pema shooed her sisters away, pushing them in the directions of the trees.

Night owls hooted from their perch and crickets sang

while the moon shone brightly. Pema closed her eyes and titled her head back, absorbing power from the silver rays. The crunch of dead leaves brought her head down and her eyes open. Claire was crossing the park and had stopped about thirty feet from her, suspicion written all over her face.

"Where is Ronan? What have you done with him? He asked me to meet him here," Claire snapped, her anger blazing like a sun in the midnight sky. With her pinched features, she looked more like her mother than ever. The only things missing were Cele's glasses and tight bun.

What the hell did this witch have to be angry about? She was the one who had tried to poison Pema, and blew up Black Moon in an attempt to kill her. Pema was the one with reasons to be pissed.

"Ronan isn't coming, I'm the one who texted you. We have things to settle. I know it was you that poisoned my drink and planted the bomb in my car. Did you really think you would get away with that?" She watched the female closely, but Claire betrayed nothing. Pema couldn't help but wonder what Ronan had seen in her. She scowled all the time and snapped at anyone who tried to engage her in conversation. She had never been pleasant or friendly to talk to, and was extremely self-centered. There was nothing attractive about her.

Claire's voice shrilled, "You have no proof of any of that. I was nowhere near Black Moon last night. I was with my mother. Have you considered one of the many other people who don't like you? It may be difficult to narrow the field down. If this is the only reason I am here, then I'm leaving."

Pema fisted her hands and placed them on her hips to keep from closing the distance and decking Claire. Suddenly, Isis' idea sounded sublime, but she had to keep it together and coax her into the circle. She wasn't going to stoop to Claire's level. She told herself to stick to the plan. "Asking your mother would be a waste of time. She's always cleaned up your messes. That's the weakest alibi I've ever heard. You can admit what you did because we both know what this is really about. You've been jealous of me since I was a baby. That's pathetic when you think about it. Being jealous of a powerless, little baby. Your attempt to kill me has failed, twice. And I'm not going anywhere, not unless my Fated Mate goes with me," Pema purred, watching shock and anger cross Claire's pinched features.

"Yeah, that's right. Ronan is mine, he belongs to me," Pema declared, relishing Claire's outrage.

Claire sputtered and stammered, her face turning red. "The Goddess would never bless, or in your case, curse, a male with you as a mate. You were a wretched, poor baby, and you are a wretched adult. I have never understood why the realm went on and on about how you and your sisters were going to take the throne and reshape magic. It was sickening to watch powerful witches and wizards fawn over a bunch of striplings in rags," she spat.

Pema was momentarily stunned silent. It was only two years ago that she had reached maturity and left her underprivileged stripling years behind. She remembered feeling inferior, and hated the cloud that being poor had cast over her. Claire was born with a silver spoon in her mouth, and had no idea what it meant to work for what you had.

Pema and her sisters had been forced to find work in the human sector to have anything. They had worked triple time to open their shop, and this witch had taken enough from them.

"That must have been a hard pill to swallow, being overshadowed by us peons when you were being groomed to take over. You don't have enough talent to rule, and my guess is that your mother knows that. You were jealous that my sisters and I rocked the rags and had the guys flocking to us regardless of what we wore," Pema laughed, taunting her to lure her closer to the circle.

Claire screamed and took a few steps forward before she regained control. Dammit, she was almost in place. Pema would need to work harder to bait her.

"You may have pretty clothes and a fancy car now, but no matter how much perfume you spray on a pile of shit, it's still just a pile of shit," Claire retorted.

Pema ignored her words. "You are a bold-faced liar. I have many things you want, talent, power, the respect of the realm, and beauty. Oh, and let's not forget…Ronan. That is why you came here, after all." Pema watched Claire's fury darken her eyes and she took another step forward. She was almost to the edge of the circle. "It must be eating you alive to know that he belongs to me. He will share my bed and my life. You will never have him again. And, your attempts on my life were laughable. You couldn't even kill me. Surely, you can do better than that."

Claire screamed out obscenities and charged. "My attempts aren't laughable. I almost had you. If Jace hadn't been there that night, you'd be dead. I have no idea how you survived the blast, but you won't survive this time!"

Pema put her hand on her wand at the small of her back and stood her ground. The enraged female crossed into their circle, activating the spell with a brilliant flash. She continued forward, lost to her anger and bounced off the outer edge, inches from Pema.

Isis and Suvi came out from their hiding spots with Suvi holding her cell phone. The three of them pulled their wands out and entered the circle. Claire's eyes widened at the sight. They formed a V with Pema at the head of the formation, closest to Claire who had whipped out her wand, pointing it at them.

"Stay back. Get away from me!" Claire shrilled.

Pema eyed her sisters before turning back to see that Claire's eyes had taken on a wild look. The witch's fear was palpable. She was unfairly out-gunned and didn't stand a chance against the three of them. Pema felt bad for her, but brushed her empathy aside. The female had tried to kill her and didn't deserve her consideration.

Still, she wasn't one to take unfair advantage. That was something Claire would do. "This is my fight. Don't engage," Pema told her sisters and re-focused on Claire. "It's just you and me. Let's see who is more powerful, shall we?"

Claire squared her shoulders and met Pema's determined gaze. "This'll be easy. I'm far more powerful." Claire pointed her wand and muttered a spell before Pema could respond. Silver sparks shot from the wand and flew towards Pema's chest. Pema fell to the ground, her heart skipped several beats as the charge went through her and she gritted her teeth against the pain. Her hand wavered, but she was able to keep her wand trained on Claire. She uttered a counter spell that sailed past Claire's shoulder.

When Claire ducked, Pema jumped up and the two of them began circling each other. Isis and Suvi followed behind Pema. When Claire tripped over a twig, Pema cast a spell. The blue light hit Claire high on her shoulder, making her cry out.

"Is that all you've got? A kitten hits harder," Claire taunted as she lobbed an amethyst sphere of energy at Pema. It hit her in the side, stealing her breath. Panting, Pema tossed another spell that landed on Claire's thigh. They went round and round lobbing spells back and forth.

Some hit their mark, causing sharp pain, while others hit the ground, causing the earth to shake.

Pema was tiring, and needed to be recharged. She reached back to Suvi as Isis' hand was on her shoulder the moment she twined fingers with Suvi, linking the three of them. A familiar hum of power arched through them and a storm brewed in the sky above. The winds picked up and debris swirled all around them.

Claire's eyes flared with panic, but she wasn't giving up, it seemed. The fever never left her midnight orbs. "You may be his mate, but that won't mean anything after I make him love me. And, trust me, he always made love to me. He didn't just stand there and fuck me like an animal!"

Oh no she didn't, Pema thought as her anger instantly spiraled out of her control. She pulled her hands free and lifted her wand to Claire. She felt Suvi and Isis reach out to her, but she was tired of this witch. Ominous clouds obscured the moon and lighting struck the ground outside their circle, illuminating the area. Sheets of rain began pouring from the sky as thunder rolled, echoing the storm within Pema. "*Dichuimhneatum*," Pema roared above the tempest, releasing all of her fury.

Claire stiffened and her eyes rolled back in her head before her body crumpled to the ground. Pema was panting and sweat beaded her brow, despite being drenched from the rain. She approached the unconscious female and prodded her with a foot. Claire didn't respond. Instead, her body began convulsing and her arms drew up to her chest as lightning rained around them. Pema glanced back at her sisters in panic. What the hell had she done?

CHAPTER 13

Tears brimmed Ronan's eyes as Hayden muttered the words of his mating ceremony to Pema, bonding Ronan and Pema for eternity. It had been a long week since the night Pema had attacked Claire. He was still angry that Pema had gone behind his back and confronted Claire, but despite this, he was proud of her. His mate acted with courage and had proved her power.

He knew Cele wanted revenge for Pema obliterating Claire's mind. Pema hadn't intended it, but she had rendered Claire brain-dead. They would deal with Cele together when she decided to seek retribution. That was one promise he squeezed out of his mate before they agreed on a date for their ceremony.

Shaking those troubling thoughts aside, he gazed at Pema and thanked the Goddess for such a priceless gift. He was the luckiest male in the Tehrex Realm. His mate never ceased to amaze him. In a matter of days, she and her sisters had gotten Black Moon up and running again *and* planned their mating.

A hot wash of pain flared in his mate mark, making him

glad the ceremony was almost done. The thought had his bear anxious to claim every inch of his mate. Ronan's blood heated at the lascivious bent of his thoughts, knowing what he would do soon. He took a deep, calming breath that was anything but, as he caught the scent of his little witch's arousal.

His resulting growl was cut off by Hayden's deep voice. "I bless this mating under the Sun and the Moon. This circle of love and honour is open and never broken, so may it be." Hayden raised their clasped hands to their group of friends and family. Enveloping warmth flooded Ronan at the pronouncement.

∽

PEMA STOOD in awe as the final words of her mating were spoken. A vibration left the mating stone and traveled from her hand and down her arm. She felt both souls leave her body and enter the stone. She looked up to their clasped hands and saw a golden light flash between their fingers. Her skin tingled with the invigorating magic. She automatically absorbed some of that magic, infusing it with her own. The connection she felt to Ronan solidified into thick golden bands joining them.

She rubbed the warmth in her chest and glanced down. It was like a cocoon of chain mail surrounded her, bringing with it a sense of peace and fulfillment.

In a flash of brilliance, their combined souls flowed back into her body, causing her to gasp. Her eyes never left Ronan's and she saw her bliss and amazement mirrored back at her. She felt the bond between them sink anchors into her completed soul.

To say she felt whole underscored the enormity of what

she experienced, and it warmed her heart to see that Ronan felt the same. She explored her soul and was awed to discover that it had been so entwined with Ronan's during the mating that a part of both resided within her. She knew everything he felt and thought. It was overwhelming, but truly remarkable, nonetheless.

Her heart raced as she felt the magic of their mating cement. The lights continued to flare through their joined hands, creating a brilliant strobe effect. The vibration intensified and was followed by a sharp pain in her palm. What was with the pain involved in a mating? First, the unrelenting pain in her mate mark, and now this. She was more than ready for the pleasure.

Having the ability to sense her discomfort, Ronan cupped her cheek and lowered his lips to hers, kissing her deeply. The pain, while intense, faded to the background as arousal quickly built to crowd it out. He poured all his love and desire into his kiss, and long moments later, they separated to loud whoops and hollers.

Her sisters and parents crowded around them. Reluctantly, she released Ronan's hand and went to give him their mating stone to protect. "Oh my Goddess," she looked at her hand, noticing the stone was a perfect chocolate diamond, and was imbedded into her palm. She lifted her head and met Ronan's stunned eyes then turned to her mother and sisters.

"What is this? You said it would be a stone we had to keep safe," she asked her mother.

"Daughter, you are special. I cannot explain the why of it, but trust that the Goddess has a plan and there is a reason. In any event, it couldn't be in a safer location," her mother reassured. She hugged her mother, glad that she had finally reached out to her. She had been so angry and had refused to listen to her mother's side.

After meeting Ronan, she understood why her mother wasn't able to deny her Fated Mate. They had spoken several times, and Pema had found a new comradery with her mother that she was coming to cherish.

Her father stepped around her mother and wrapped his arm around her. "Your mother is right. I am so proud of you. I love you, sweetheart. Congratulations," he kissed her cheek.

Pema grabbed a hold of him and whispered into his ear. "I know you have had a rough time, but your mate is out there and you too will find this extraordinary love."

When she pulled back, she saw the tears in his eyes along with a glimmer of hope. He nodded to her and gave her over to the barrage of people waiting.

It seemed like forever before she was in Ronan's arms again. They took to the dance floor of Confetti Too where the ceremony had taken place. She gazed up at her mate and felt her heart swell with her love. "I love you, Ronan."

He grabbed her ass and pulled her into the line of his body. "I love you too, mate. And, I need to be inside you before I lose my mind," he growled.

"Mmm hmm," she agreed. "So, how long until we can be alone?" she asked and kissed him. She heard his breath hitch and his pine scent intensified.

"We can sneak off to our room anytime you want. Tell me you want to go now," he husked. The reminder of the first time they had sex in the backroom sent fire racing through Pema's blood.

"Goddess yes, now," she murmured against his lips. He picked her up and walked toward the back without ever breaking contact or looking back at their guests. She hiked her dress up and wrapped her legs around his hips.

He shifted his hold on her and turned the knob, throwing a door open. She turned her head and gasped at what she saw. The large, silk-covered bed took up most of the room, which was now filled with wild flowers and hundreds of candles that lit the room, casting flickering shadows on the walls. "Oh, wow." She met his eyes, touched beyond words by his thoughtfulness.

"I wanted this to be perfect," he declared.

He had done so much to show her she was cherished and she wanted to reciprocate. She unwrapped her legs and slid slowly down his body. She placed her hands on his hips. "You mean the world to me, Ronan. Let me show you how much I love you." She reached for his button and popped it open.

∼

Ronan watched as she undid his trousers and slid them to his ankles. She remained on her knees before him, a breath away from his straining cock. Unequivocally, she was the most beautiful and sensual female ever created. The sight nearly undid him. He was anxious for the blood exchange that would finalize their mating, but he wasn't going to stop her...yet.

Having her eyes on his shaft made it harden even more, pre-cum leaking from the tip. Her tongue snaked out and licked at her lower lip. Little devil was anxious to taste him. Sexiest thing ever. She looked up while that tongue extended the millimeter to taste him. His knees locked as pleasure exploded through his shaft. Her tiny fist wrapped around his prodigious length and stroked him.

"Love, you are killing me. Suck it into that hot little mouth."

One corner of her mouth curled up in a smile before she obliged by opening her lips and sucking the nerve-laden head into her mouth. She took him all the way to the back of her throat, sending sensations exploding through his senses. "Fuck!" he cried out as she sucked him hard. "Goddess, you keep that up and I will explode in your mouth."

He smelled her spike in arousal at his words and his animal stirred, aching to claim her fully. If he let his bear have its way, he would take her dark passage. Ronan wouldn't let that happen before the blood exchange, but later, he promised. Tonight was about cementing their bond. His thoughts scattered when she pumped her hand up and down his length as she sucked him. His hands flew into her hair and he found his hips thrusting with her ministrations.

He tried to withdraw before it was too late, knowing she was turned on and aching too, but she refused to allow him to move. She reached under her dress and slipped her hand into her own panties. She moaned against him as she touched herself. "Let me go, I need to taste you." She shook her head and brought her hand out, thrusting her fingers into his mouth. He licked them clean. His mate was not a shy one and that turned his blood to lava in his veins.

"Enough," he barked and withdrew from her. He picked her up and threw her to the bed. "I can't wait to be inside you. I will be as gentle as possible, but you have me in a frenzy," he rushed out as he lifted the skirt of her dress and ripped off her panties.

"I don't want gentle, Ronan. Let your animal out. Fuck me hard and fast."

He pulled the top of her dress down, exposing her breasts. Desire overrode all else. He had to have her or he would die. It would always be like this with her, he realized. This intense, overwhelming passion. And, he couldn't be happier.

"You aren't ready for my bear. Soon...but not tonight." He kissed her, stopping her protests. His tongue moved over hers, fanning the flames higher. He ran his hands up the sides of her body, pinching her nipples along the way. He kissed between her breasts and down to the soft flesh between her legs. Too amped up, he wasted no time in running his tongue from her core to her bundle of nerves. He sucked her clit into his mouth, tasting the heat and need flaming through her. His tongue licked her opening, loving the sweet summer strawberries. It was an aphrodisiac to his senses.

"I need more Ronan. Give me more, dammit," she demanded.

Beyond words, he rose over her and pressed his cock against the swollen folds of her pussy. She was so damned wet for him. He rubbed his length along her slit, coating his cock with her juices. He pulled his hips back then inch by inch he sank into *Annwyn*. He felt her tightening and clenching around him like a slick, wet fist.

"You are so hot and tight. Goddess, it's an exquisite agony," he declared. At that moment, he wanted to do as she had asked and let his bear loose to fuck them both into a violent release. In fact, he wasn't sure he could stop that from happening. The desire for the blood exchange was the only thing that stopped him.

He pulled out and thrust back in slowly, enjoying the delicious torture. "This is only the appetizer. The main course will come when we get home. As much as I'd love to stay here making love to you all night, we do have friends and family waiting for us," he grunted and punctuated his point with a hard lunge back into her tightness. She milked him and sucked him greedily back in.

She raised her head and sucked one of his nipples into her mouth, catching him off guard, while at the same time, reaching between their bodies and grabbing his balls. He cried out and nearly lost his seed right there. Naughty little witch. It took all his strength, but he continued his slow pace.

She gave his balls another squeeze and bit his nipple. That broke his will and a growl left him. He began pumping into her hot body while her pussy clamped down. She was close and he reached between their bodies, finding her clit. He pinched the engorged nub between his thumb and forefinger. She exploded around him and he felt his incisors elongate.

"You are mine. Now and always. I will cherish you the rest of my life and beyond. Are you ready for the blood exchange?" She rippled around him, clearly excited at the idea. For supernaturals, the mating was solidified during the blood exchange and Ronan was dying with anticipation. He was on the verge of climax, but holding back for that moment.

"I have never been more ready for anything in my life," she said, panting and coming down from her peak.

"I love you," he said as he licked the crook of her neck, teasing the flesh, making her pulse hammer. He groaned when she released his balls and grabbed his shoulders, pulling her body up. She sank her blunt teeth into his shoulder, making him cry out before he returned the favor and sank his canines into her delicate flesh. The moment her blood hit his tongue, his cock swelled, locking him inside her writhing pussy as they both exploded.

As their climaxes tore through them, he felt the final

link of their mating click into place. She came hard, muttering something he scarcely heard through the haze. An exquisite pleasure-pain that only served to intensify his release flowed from the spot she had bitten on his neck. He let it wash over him and all but collapsed on top of her after they were both spent.

Sweat covered both their bodies and she was panting as hard as he was. He rolled to the side, separating their bodies and pulled her into his embrace. She lifted her arm, inspecting her mating mark. He glanced at his own and realized that the brand was now inked into his skin like a tattoo. He laid his arm next to hers, seeing they matched.

In the distance they heard, voices echoing from their mating celebration. His body was replete for a moment in time until his sexy little witch wiggled her delectable ass against his groin, waking it up. "That was so beyond incredible. I want to say forget the rest of them and stay in here with you all night, but I suppose we need to get back to the party," she murmured.

"Witch, you can't wiggle that fine ass up against me and expect I'm not going to take it. The party *will* wait," he growled and kissed her passionately.

∾

ANOTHER LIGHT BULB exploded overhead and a tear trickled down Cele's cheek. She was furious at those Rowan triplets and if she didn't need their power, they would all be dead already. They had destroyed her legacy, and taken everything that mattered from her.

Brushing a stray hair from her daughter's forehead, she choked back her emotion. She once again chanted a restoration spell, but Claire remained unresponsive. There was nothing left, but the shell of her beautiful Claire. To look at her daughter now broke her heart. Once so full of life, Claire now sat powerless to her body and mind, with drool dripping down her chin and her hands turned inward and curled up against her chest.

Cele turned away as the nurse entered the room to take care of her daughter, vowing that the Rowans would suffer for what they had done.

EXCERPT FROM ISIS' BETRAYAL, DARK WARRIOR ALLIANCE BOOK 4

"If I have to hear that bear growl one more freakin' time, I'm going to paralyze his vocal cords. Goddess, do they ever come up for air?" Isis asked, unable to curb her irritation any longer.

"Not since the mating ceremony," Suvi laughed. "Come on, sis, Pema deserves this happiness." Isis watched the youngest of her sisters closely, envying her levity.

"I know she does, and you're right, but I feel the walls closing in on me. Let's go to Confetti Too," Isis said. She had contemplated moving out over the past few days, but in the end, she knew that wasn't an option. Unlike humans, supernaturals didn't thrive from independence. Supernaturals prospered when they lived with family and friends; whereas, lone individuals tended to wither away.

Isis looked over and noticed Suvi was typing out a text. Before her eyes lifted from the phone, it chirped. "I'm in. The Dark Warriors are going to be there. C'mon you, need to put on something sexier. And, we need to leave some food outside Pema's door before we leave." Suvi's musical voice was filled with excitement and Isis couldn't help but get excited about the evening, too.

Isis resisted Suvi's prodding and smoothed her hair down. "I'll go, but I'm not changing. These are my favorite jeans, and, what's wrong with this top?" Isis asked, examining her clothing. It was a stylish top and she'd gotten several compliments on her tight, hip-hugging jeans in the past.

Suvi reached out and undid the top two buttons of her green shirt. "What's wrong, sister, is that you need to flash more cleavage."

Isis rolled her eyes and headed for the back door. "I don't need to flash my shit to get attention. In fact, a little lesson for you, males like a little mystery. Make them use their imagination, work for it. No one wants what they can see. Half the excitement for them is the fantasy they create about you in their head," she smiled and winked at her sister.

"Well, I'm changing. I've never had anyone complain about the way I look. In fact, less is more," Suvi chuckled with her reply as she headed for the stairs. Isis followed her up to the second floor where the noise of hot-shifter-on-witch sex was getting louder.

Isis glanced down at her crinkle-chiffon top and thought about changing as well, but decided against it because she wanted to get out of the house sooner, rather than, later. Suvi's dress choice was always well-put together, but she hoped she didn't take too long.

As they walked into Suvi's room, Isis had never been more thankful for being a witch than she had been since Pema was mated. Witches' hearing wasn't as strong as other immortals, so she wasn't able to pick up the minute sounds of their lovemaking like she would if she were a vampire or shifter. She laughed aloud thinking of the paybacks for

Ronan when she or Suvi finally found her Fated Mate. He'd be able to hear everything.

Her mind wandered to the Dark Warriors, and she idly wondered if their rooms were soundproofed to muffle the noise. She surmised that it could get testy in that house with a bunch of un-mated males and two mated couples. One thing she had come to learn, since the mating phenomenon had returned to the Tehrex Realm, was that Fated Mates were combustible together.

Isis wasn't like her sister, Pema, who hadn't wanted her Fated Mate. Pema and Ronan had had their work cut out for them before they were officially mated. Ronan's ex-girlfriend, Claire, had tried to kill Pema twice, and Pema had to work through her biases to eventually accept Ronan. Just the thought of what Claire had done to Pema had Isis' anger flaring and, instantly, several lightbulbs in the ceiling burst. As tiny shards of glass went flying, she quickly tamped it down before any more damage was done.

"You okay?" Suvi turned around, eyeing her warily.

"I'm good. So why isn't that red dress good enough for you to wear?"

"Because I've had it on all day and I want to wear this new purple one I just picked up. I have a cute, little green dress that will look better than your jeans," Suvi tried again to convince her to change. Isis watched Suvi toss clothes out of her closet as she searched for something to wear.

Isis wasn't against dressing up, or wearing clothes that others might consider revealing, but she didn't feel the need to make a production out of every outing. She already felt sexy in what she was wearing, so she didn't feel the need to change. She sat down at Suvi's vanity and glanced in the mirror, admitting she could touch up her make-up, though.

Suvi came out of the closet holding up two dresses. "I

think you should wear the green one, because it will look great with your red hair, but the blue would look amazeballs on you, too. Here, try it on."

"I'm not changing, Suvi. I like what I have on," Isis gritted out, trying to hold back her frustration before it turned to anger. She turned back to the mirror and finished with her eye make-up.

"Okay, point taken. You know I can't help myself when it comes to clothes and shoes. Oooh, nice smoky eyes. Try this shimmery lip-gloss." Isis smiled at Suvi in the mirror. True to form, nothing much ruffled Suvi's feathers.

The three of them perfectly balanced each other, but Isis was having a hard time adjusting to the changes in dynamics that Ronan had created. Their mating was for the best, and she would never want Pema to be without the bear, but things were definitely different in Casa de Rowan. Normally, Pema would have been getting ready with them and joining them for a night out. One third of the power of three had been missing lately.

Suvi stripped out of her red dress and poured herself into a slinky little purple number. The garment was one of the shortest dresses she had ever seen. "Suvi, you had better not bend over tonight. I know you don't mind showing the males your assets, but I don't think you need to flash them your black thong."

A loud roar from the next room had them looking at one another. "Time to go," they said in unison and burst out laughing.

They quickly headed downstairs. "You're free to roam the house naked for a couple hours. We're heading to Confetti," Suvi called out as they passed Pema's door.

"There are leftovers in the fridge, but don't you dare touch my piece of key lime pie or I'll pound your ass," Isis threatened, meaning every word. No one touched her favorite dessert and lived to tell about it.

They ignored Pema's muffled reply and Isis grabbed the keys to the Audi off the hook by the back door and tossed them over her shoulder. "You're driving, bitch," she winked at Suvi.

~

"Oh Goddess, here comes Plain Paula," Isis leaned over and whispered to Suvi. "Whatever you do, don't let her talk about her personal-training bullshit...like anyone cares. Doesn't she realize we don't need to exercise? Apparently not, since she never shuts up once she gets started. Boring as hell." Supernaturals were naturally fit and didn't need to exercise to maintain it, but that wasn't to say that most didn't have a daily regimen they followed. Some, more than others, she thought, ruefully.

Suvi held back her laughter, snorting her drink into her nose. "Crap, that burns. And, we can't avoid her now, here she comes."

"Hey there, how are you two? It's odd to see you without Pema. How does she like mated life? Don't you just love the new club?" Paula asked as she reached their table. Isis was shocked the super-short nymph stopped talking long enough to catch her breath.

"Hey Pl...Paula. We're great and Pema is superbly happy. Mating like bunnies as we speak," Suvi said, her musical voice an invitation Isis didn't want her to deliver.

"You know, sex burns five calories per minute, so, if they have sex for five hours, they have burned fifteen hundred calories. Of course, on my ten-mile hike today, which I did in less than two hours, I burned sixteen hundred and ten calories. See," Plain Paula pulled out her cell phone and began pushing buttons, "this FabFit app keeps track for me. I can even post it to my TRex page. And, then I did twenty-four reps on my weight circuit and burned another thousand calories."

Isis was supremely glad that she hadn't accepted Paula's sup-connect. She had no desire to see this female's hourly caloric burn. The TRex page was the supernatural social media. Humans thought they invented such ways to connect, when truth was, Killian, a Dark Alliance council member and owner of Confetti Too, developed it at least two decades before. Even supernaturals fell victim to vanity and used their pages to flaunt what they had and make others jealous. Difference was, the public bulletins usually involved demons and skirm attacks.

When the Vampire King, Zander, was blessed with his Fated Mate several months ago, breaking the mating curse, the feeds went crazy with the news. Isis remembered reading about it, thinking the realm's reaction was overkill. She and her sisters were young, she realized, and maybe unable to appreciate the full impact of going without mate blessings for over seven hundred years.

The lapse had led to all sorts of changes the realm had never seen before, such as the Adorned. Adorned were the children of unmated couples and were extremely rare. Being one of a set of Adorned triplets was even more rare and made her and her sisters subjects of a long-ago prophesy. Children of any kind had been scarce over the spanning centuries. Of course, there were some previously-mated couples having children, but the Tehrex Realm population had dipped drastically.

Having spent time with the Dark Warriors and members of the Dark Alliance council, Isis better understood the importance of this decline in population, especially considering the war they had been waging against the archdemons for centuries.

Isis shuddered at the thought of the archdemons and their skirm and the destruction they were capable of causing. She and her sisters owned a shop where they sold magical accoutrements, potions, and did tarot reading for both supernaturals and humans. Black Moon had seen its share of devastated individuals in their store searching for ways to help their loved ones heal from injuries or ones looking for ways to ease the grieving process.

Suvi's voice intruded into Isis' musings. "How many calories would they have burned if they'd been fucking for three days straight?" Isis wanted to smack her sister upside the head for encouraging Paula. They'd never get rid of her at this rate.

Plain Paula cocked her head to the side and considered for a fraction of a second, oblivious to the fact that Suvi was poking fun at her. "Approximately twenty-one thousand, six hundred calories. Now, that's a serious workout. You need to come down to my gym and let me put you through the paces. You'll feel like new witches."

"Och, female. Are you really a nymph? I canna understand how you think of nothing but your exercise," Bhric harangued as he approached the table.

They turned their heads and ogled the six-foot-three, drop-dead gorgeous, Vampire Prince. His amber eyes gleamed with humor as he ran a hand through his buzzed hair. She heard Suvi inhale sharply and understood the feeling. He was a fine specimen with his bulging muscles, black leather pants, and tight blue t-shirt. Not to mention, Isis loved his thick, Scottish bur.

Isis was certain Plain Paula was about to begin another

diatribe about the benefits of being a personal trainer, but Bhric saved them. "Come, my lovely lasses, let's dance."

Isis eagerly jumped up and grabbed her sister's hand, following the big, burly warrior onto the dance floor while Plain Paula called out to their retreating backs, "You know dancing is another great way to burn calories."

"That female is a wee bit obsessive aboot the exercise, is she no'? 'Tis disturbing and most definitely no' natural. Her da must have been human," Bhric observed as he turned to them when they reached the middle of the floor.

A smile spread across Isis' face, thinking obsessive was too mild a description. "Thanks for saving us. I almost grabbed the gun from my purse and shot her between the eyes."

Bhric shimmied his hips and sauntered closer to them. The male really was a sexy beast and was built like a brick house. "Ah, lass, my motives are no' entirely selfless. I plan to have you both pay me back." He waggled his eyebrows, making Isis laugh.

"I'm happy to pay you anything you want," Suvi replied, gyrating against the prince. Her little sister had a thing for vampires and Isis was certain she would be happy to take one, or ten, for the team.

Isis shook her head and threw her hands up, quickly losing herself in the music. She jumped and wiggled and moved her hips, having a blast. She and Suvi danced close to Bhric, arousing the Prince, if his erection was any indication. She stepped back into Bhric and rubbed her backside against his groin while her sister stood behind him caressing him. Suvi maneuvered her way in front of Bhric and they continued their movements. The dancing ended when her sister cupped Bhric through his pants.

When the growling and nipping started, Isis left the

dance floor, heading to a table far away from Plain Paula. She was hot and sweaty, needing a drink, and rethinking her stubborn choice to wear jeans given they were sticking to her skin.

She lifted her long hair off her neck and scanned the room for any of the other Dark Warriors, especially Rhys. Her body had been amped up since she entered the club, and Rhys, a cambion, would be just the ticket to sate her need.

While Suvi had a thing for vampires, Isis enjoyed a cambion. They were the offspring of a human and a sex demon and had many sensual powers. Given that they needed sex frequently to keep their strength, they were always searching for someone, and all that experience made them incredible lovers. They were notorious creatures of heat, fun and passion, all three of which she needed at the moment.

She didn't see the Dark Warriors, so she headed for the far bar and ordered a vodka tonic. Isis turned her back to the bar and leaned against it with her foot propped on the stool next to her. She contemplated re-buttoning her shirt as it pulled tight across her breasts when she rested her elbows behind her. A surreptitious check told her that her breasts were spilling out of her black bra. Given the sheen of sweat on her skin, she decided to unbutton a couple more instead. When she looked up, a particularly sexy male caught her attention. They locked eyes, staring at one another for several moments, before he began walking toward her.

Authors' Note

With new digital download trends, authors rely on readers to spread the word more than ever. Here are some ways to help us.

Leave a review! Every author asks their readers to take five minutes and let others know how much you enjoyed their work. Here's the reason why. Reviews help your favorite authors to become visible. It's simple and easy to do. If you are a Kindle user turn to the last page and leave a review before you close your book. For other retailers, just visit their online site and leave a brief review.

Don't forget to visit our website: www.trimandjulka.com and sign up for our newsletter, which is jam-packed with exciting news and monthly giveaways. Also, be sure to visit and like our Facebook page https://www.facebook.com/TrimAndJulka to see our daily themes, including hot guys, drink recipes and book teasers.

Trust your journey and remember that the future is yours and it's filled with endless possibilities!

DREAM BIG!

XOXO,

Brenda & Tami

OTHER WORKS BY TRIM AND JULKA
The Dark Warrior Alliance
Dream Warrior (Dark Warrior Alliance, Book One)
Mystik Warrior (Dark Warrior Alliance, Book Two)
Pema's Storm (Dark Warrior Alliance, Book Three)
Deviant Warrior (Dark Warrior Alliance, Book Four)
Isis' Betrayal (Dark Warrior Alliance, Book Five)
Suvi's Revenge (Dark Warrior Alliance, Book Six)
Mistletoe & Mayhem (Dark Warrior Alliance, Book 6.5)
Scarred Warrior (Dark Warrior Alliance, Book Seven)
Heat in the Bayou (Dark Warrior Alliance, Novella, Book 7.5)
Hellbound Warrior (Dark Warrior Alliance, Book Eight)
Isobel (Dark Warrior Alliance, Book Nine)
Rogue Warrior (Dark Warrior Alliance, Book Ten)
Tinsel & Temptation (Dark Warrior Alliance, Book 10.5)
Shattered Warrior (Dark Warrior Alliance, Book Eleven)
King of Khoth (Dark Warrior Alliance, Book Twelve)

The Rowan Sisters' Trilogy

The Rowan Sisters' Trilogy Boxset (Books 1-3)

Don't miss out!
Click the button below and you can sign up to receive emails from Trim and Julka about new releases, fantastic giveaways, and their latest hand made jewelry. There's no charge and no obligation.

Printed in Great Britain
by Amazon